Readers love ANDREW GREY

The Gift

"*The Gift* was sexy, passionate, and emotional and such a fun ride... Thank you for another fantastic, fun read Mr. Grey. You never cease to amaze me..."

—MM Good Book Reviews

"Mr. Grey has given us a wonderful story of love and hope and I hope you each grab a copy and enjoy."

—House of Millar

A Spirit Without Borders

"Nobody writes like Andrew Grey. I pick up one of his books and start reading, and I can't put it down. This one definitely was one of those books."

—Inked Rainbow Reads

Saving Faithless Creek

"I loved it! This was such a sweet story, I couldn't help but fall in love! This is a must read!"

—Boundless Book Reviews

"*Saving Faithless Creek* is a sweet romance and a journey of self-discovery... beautiful story and one fans of this author will not want to miss."

—Joyfully Jay

By ANDREW GREY

Accompanied by a Waltz
Between Loathing and Love
Crossing Divides
Dominant Chord
Dutch Treat
Eastern Cowboy
In Search of a Story
North to the Future
One Good Deed
Path Not Taken
Saving Faithless Creek
Shared Revelations
Stranded • Taken
Three Fates (Multiple Author Anthology)
To Have, Hold, and Let Go
Whipped Cream

HOLIDAY STORIES
Copping a Sweetest Day Feel • Cruise for Christmas
A Lion in Tails • Mariah the Christmas Moose
A Present in Swaddling Clothes • Simple Gifts
Snowbound in Nowhere • Stardust

ART
Legal Artistry • Artistic Appeal • Artistic Pursuits • Legal Tender

BOTTLED UP
The Best Revenge • Bottled Up • Uncorked • An Unexpected Vintage

BRONCO'S BOYS
Inside Out • Upside Down • Backward

THE BULLRIDERS
A Wild Ride • A Daring Ride • A Courageous Ride

BY FIRE
Redemption by Fire • Strengthened by Fire • Burnished by Fire • Heat Under Fire

CARLISLE COPS
Fire and Water
Fire and Ice

Published by DREAMSPINNER PRESS
www.dreamspinnerpress.com

Published by DREAMSPINNER PRESS
www.dreamspinnerpress.com

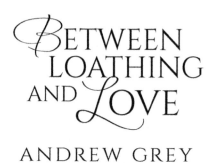

BETWEEN LOATHING AND LOVE

ANDREW GREY

Published by

DREAMSPINNER PRESS

5032 Capital Circle SW, Suite 2, PMB# 279, Tallahassee, FL 32305-7886 USA
www.dreamspinnerpress.com

Between Loathing and Love
© 2015 Andrew Grey.

Cover Art
© 2015 L.C. Chase.
http://www.lcchase.com
Cover content is for illustrative purposes only and any person depicted on the cover is a model.

ISBN: 978-1-63476-633-3
Digital ISBN: 978-1-63476-634-0
Library of Congress Control Number: 2015942999
First Edition October 2015

Printed in the United States of America
∞
This paper meets the requirements of
ANSI/NISO Z39.48-1992 (Permanence of Paper).

For Dominic, because I can't work, eat, sleep, or exist without him.

CHAPTER 1—LOATHING

LOATHING WAS not an emotion I felt all that often. I really liked to think I was a nice guy who tended to get along with others, but some days were trying beyond belief, and right at this moment, I found I couldn't stand to be in the office for a single minute longer. My boss had made me angry, but I didn't really loathe the man—that was way too strong a word. There was one person on earth who I could definitively put in that category, and my boss didn't come close to him. Not that I'd thought about that asshole in years, so why the hell was I going down that path? I needed to get a grip.

I had dreamed of a career in show business. I hadn't figured it would be on the theatrical-agent side of the curtain, but what could I do? I had just been hired and relocated from central Michigan to New York. A dream come true, or so I had thought at the time. I loved New York, and the job I'd landed was a very good one. I'd even managed to sublet an apartment in the Village through a friend of a friend for surprisingly reasonable rent.

"Payton," my friend Val—short for Valentine—called as he bounced down the street in my direction, while I stood huddled in the doorway of the gym to stay out of the gale-force cold wind blowing from the East River toward the Hudson. I clutched my gym bag in my hand, hoping like hell my hand didn't freeze and fall off. "You made it."

"Yeah," I grumbled. "I thought I'd landed a new client, but my boss, the dick from hell, decided that even though I'd done most of the work, it was really Garren's find, so he got the client and I'm out in the cold… again. How was I supposed to know Garren had already approached him?" I followed him inside and checked in at the desk before heading to the locker rooms.

"Let it go, Pay," he chirped in that way he had that made the worst problem seem stupid and overdramatic. "You'll get 'em next time. Did your boss give you any credit at all?"

"Yeah, he did," I answered, letting go of some of my anger at the man. "He said I did a great job with follow-up and determination. Then he handed the client over to that sleazeball Garren."

"Was that shudder drama or real?" Val teased as he pulled open locker after locker until he found the one he wanted. Val had this ritual where he never took the first locker available and always had to open the empty ones until he found one that seemed just right. Not that I could ever tell the difference. I asked him last week about it, and he'd looked at me like I was crazy. I actually didn't think he realized was doing it. "Because if it's drama, knock it off. This is a gym, not a theater," Val went on as though he hadn't paused. "If it's real, get over it. This is New York, and you got to be tough here or you'll get chewed up and spat out."

"So what's your advice, all-knowing sage?" I quipped as I took the locker Val designated as mine and began pulling off my tie.

"Honestly?" he asked. "Get the client to sign the contract and specify in it that you handle the account. Who cares then if Garren or anyone else has approached him—you're in." Val hung up his coat and shoved his shoes in the bottom of the locker before shucking his clothes faster than a stripper on a deadline. Val was a nice enough looking guy; most would say he was cute. He had the "floppy blond-haired twink" look down pat, and he was trim enough to pull it off, regardless of his actual age.

"Hey, Val," a guy said suggestively as he passed the bay of lockers wearing only a towel. I was half surprised he didn't decide it needed straightening, just to give Val a look at the goods. But given the look, Val had probably already done more than just see the goods already. Val did little more than wave slightly before pulling on his workout clothes. I finished getting my suit off and hung up, then pulled on my workout shorts and an old T-shirt. I sat on the bench to put on my shoes while Val talked briefly with another guy.

"You ready?" he asked once I had my shoes on. We went back out into the lobby to take the elevator up to the workout floor. What always surprised me was that even in a health club, no one took the stairs.

"Do you know everyone?" I asked once the doors opened and we got into the otherwise empty elevator.

"I grew up here. Everyone thinks New York is huge, and it is, but it's also neighborhoods with people you see every day. The club is like that. You'll see once you get used to it." My real friendship with Val began the first day I moved to New York, as I was moving into my teeny ground-floor apartment. He lived upstairs in a comparative palace. He'd been raised by his grandmother, and when she passed away, she left Val the apartment, which she'd owned. I'd originally met Val when he'd come to Mount Pleasant to visit relatives who lived down the street from me. He spent the summer with them, so we got to know each other pretty well, but only for that summer. Still, Val was pretty unforgettable. So when I got the job in New York, I called him and he took me under his wing, for which I would be eternally grateful.

The elevator doors opened at the weight machine floor, and a huge guy got on wearing the smallest shirt I had ever seen. It had to be made out of dental floss.

"Hi, Val," the man said as the doors closed and the elevator started up again. I had to cover my mouth to keep from laughing.

"Hi, Jerry. This is my friend Pay. He moved to the city a month ago."

Jerry turned to me, and I shook hands with the guy.

"Nice to meet you."

"Same here," Jerry said, and the elevator doors opened, letting in some fresh air. Jerry stepped out, lumbered to the nearest treadmill, and started it right up.

"Jerry's a nice guy but…." Val blew out his breath.

"He sounds like a girl," I whispered.

"Yeah," Val nodded. "He's competitive. I don't know what he's on, but the 'see Tarzan, hear Jane' thing is kind of sad. The stuff also makes them sweat like crazy." Val strode around the cardio floor until he found two step machines next to each other. Val always insisted that we start with those because of what he claimed they did for his ass. Granted, Val had a great backside, so I didn't argue and got on the machine. I started stepping and set the machine at the level I wanted, then settled in to watch the people around me.

"Aren't you glad I talked you into joining?" Val said from next to me, and I turned toward him. "There's a lot to see." He smiled and I nodded. "A lot of the guys are gay, which tends to make the place a little cruisy, but the equipment is awesome and people are pretty friendly."

"I guess."

"There's no need to be shy," Val chided and chuckled when I blushed. He'd noticed I did that and seemed to enjoy it when it happened. I blamed it on my Midwestern upbringing. Things like sex and being gay were rarely talked about. The few times my mother had ever mentioned sex to me, she'd done so in a whisper, as if the angels might hear her and punish her for it. She used the same tone whenever she mentioned what someone died of or was in the hospital for, as if those same angels would give her cancer if she said it loud enough. Sadly, maybe she had something there, because that's what she had died of just a few years ago.

"Please. With my luck I'd look at the one straight guy here and get my face beat in," I countered and went back to my workout as Val laughed at me and then struck up a conversation with the attractive, slightly older but built man next to him. I ended up watching the countdown clock on my machine until the elevator doors slid open and a man stepped out in a light blue tank top and black shorts that hugged his thighs and accentuated the curve of a Greek statue butt.

"Val," I whispered, thankful he was no longer chatting up the guy on the other side.

"What?"

"Do you know who that is? The guy in the black shorts."

Val grinned over at me. "No, but damn you got good taste." He giggled and we both followed him with our eyes as he moved around the floor. John Travolta had nothing on this guy when it came to strutting, and I watched those glutes shift up and down with each step. Of course, as soon as he turned to where he might see me, I looked away and did my best not to stare at him. But dang he was hard not to look at: tanned skin with just a hint of olive tone to it, legs I wanted to climb to get a glimpse of where they led, and shorts that hinted, loudly, that everything on him was perfectly proportional. My mouth went kind of dry for a few seconds, and I licked my lips, nearly faltering on the damn machine. I caught myself and pulled my attention back to where it needed to be. He passed by right in front of me, and I turned to Val just as I thought he might have actually glanced in my direction. By the time I turned to see if he had, I was treated to another view of his retreating backside as he made another circuit.

"He checked you out," Val whispered and nudged me with his elbow.

"He was probably looking to see how long I had left on the machine," I said logically. What did I have that could catch the attention of a smoking-hot guy like that? The place was packed and every machine was in use. In fact, some people looked as though they were getting ready to pitch tents rather than give up their machines. I was getting thirsty and wished I'd remembered a water bottle, so when my time ran out, I asked Val if he'd guard my machine so I could get a drink. I stepped off, and the guy I'd been watching made a beeline across the floor and jumped on the machine before I could open my mouth.

"I'm only getting a drink of water," I explained, but he paid no attention and started climbing.

"I need to keep my heart rate up," he said emphatically, like it was the most important thing in the world. Then he turned toward me, and I felt myself pale and then grow hot. I instantly turned on my heel and marched away, trying my best not to punch the fucking wall as I approached it.

"What's wrong?" Val asked as he hurried up behind me, pushing my wiping towel into my hand. "We were already done."

"Screw that. I know that guy," I forced between my teeth.

"From where?"

"High school. He's one of the pieces of shit who made my life miserable senior year." I tried to push away the absolute loathing I had for the man. I'd been angry at my boss, but this was deep hatred. "I thought Beckett was my friend. You know, not a close friend or anything, but we had some classes together, and unlike all the other kids, he was fairly nice." I stepped out of the aisle to give others room.

"Get your drink and then we can do some of the machines. We need to work on more than cardio," Val said. "The gorilla isn't worth getting upset over." I couldn't help smiling at the way Val glared at Beckett on my behalf. "Some people are just rude," he said loudly enough to make sure he could hear. Then, when Beckett turned in our direction, Val put his nose in the air, turned his back, and walked away, doing a dang good impression of a model walking a fashion runway. Half the guys in the place took notice. Val pushed the call button for the elevator, and by the time it arrived, we had to cram in along with the four other guys who'd answered Val's "call of the wild." Not a single one of them looked twice at me.

Val was in his element. He talked with the guys a little, soaked up their compliments, took their phone numbers when offered, and then led me out of the car and onto the floor with the weight machines. It was quieter here, and we each took a chest machine and got to work.

"I really hate that guy," I said as I sat down.

"What did he do that was so bad?" Val asked.

"Okay. It was the beginning of senior year. I was in the drama club and I liked photography, but I stayed away from the yearbook people because I didn't want to add to my nerd credentials any more than I already had. Word got to the head of the yearbook that I could take pictures." I set up the weights and began pushing the handles forward, clenching my chest muscles to get the most from the workout. Val did the same on the next machine, and when we were done, I continued. "They asked me to take pictures at one of the football games. Beckett, the gorilla upstairs, was the star quarterback, of course." I rolled my eyes. "Anyway, I went to the game and took the pictures they wanted. Then I decided I wanted to get some of the empty stands before they shut off the lights. There were some really interesting shadows," I added when Val looked at me like I was insane. "To make a long story short, I heard noises and caught Beckett getting a blowjob." I leaned closer. "From a guy. And it wasn't a 'close your eyes and imagine a girl' blowjob either. He was into it, telling Peter that he was going to fuck his hot little ass once they got home and that Peter wasn't going to come until Beckett swallowed his beefy cock. Stuff like that."

"Did you join in?" Val asked with mesmerized interest.

"No. I tried to get out of there, but Beckett saw me. I got away anyhow, and that's when he really started coming after me. His favorite taunts were 'Gaydie Paydie' or 'Pay-*ton*' because I was, like, five foot eight and weighed about two-ten at one point. I was big and clumsy, with a double chin and everything." I sat back and increased the weight, jamming the arm forward on the machine. My anger seemed to have taken over. When I was done, Val stared at me.

"You should put that energy to good use. How about kick the asshole in the nuts? If you could find them." Val was being catty on my behalf, and I really appreciated it.

"Beckett doesn't have grapes—more like grapefruits," I retorted, and then I looked at the floor. "I saw him, remember, in all his spit-slicked glory."

"Okay. So he saw you. Did you say anything?" Val asked.

"No. I pretended it never happened. I mean, I was gay too. I didn't need to make myself an even bigger target."

"So to speak."

"Shut up." I lightly smacked Val's shoulder. "Anyway, I figured it was his business, and I didn't want anyone to go through what I had, so I kept quiet and stayed away from him. Then a week later it's all over school that Beckett's gay. It was a big deal for a while, and he took a bunch of flak, but he was still the star player and he just played harder."

"You have to admire the guy for that," Val said, and I turned and growled at him. "What? You do."

"Yeah, except Beckett made my life miserable as soon as it came out. I guess he had to show everyone there were still some things worse than being gay in the high school world, like being fat. It didn't matter that at Thanksgiving I went to the doctor and they changed my asthma medication, and the weight melted away like crazy. Mom was a nurse. She helped me devise a diet I could live with, and I dropped, like, fifty pounds in four months. The old meds had apparently been messing with my metabolism, and after that I had energy and never stopped moving. The weight came off and I felt better about myself, but the teasing only got worse."

The elevator was right across from where I was sitting at the machine, and when the doors slid open I half expected Beckett to come striding out. I actually held my breath and released it when the doors closed again.

"Why?"

"I came out as gay, figuring that since people had accepted Beckett it would be no big deal. To my friends it wasn't, but Beckett only made me hate school more. He was a real piece of work." I decided to end the story there. No use going into all that right now. The elevator doors opened again, and this time Beckett strode out and around the rows of machines. I got up, found one to work my back, and got to it. I needed to keep busy and blow off the tension and anger that increased the longer he was in the room.

I knew I was being completely unreasonable. High school was six years ago, and I thought I'd moved beyond it. My college experience had been amazing—I made wonderful friends who were lining up to visit me this summer in New York. I'd made a lot of changes in my life and liked to think I had grown beyond the pettiness of adolescence. But maybe that was a little premature.

Once I finished my set, I looked around the sea of stainless steel, silver, and black, wondering where Val had gotten off to, and my gaze fell on Beckett. He was on the machine right across from me, leaning slightly back, legs splayed apart until he squeezed them together. Jesus Christ. I nearly swallowed my teeth. His shorts clung to his legs and hips so tightly they left nothing—not a single thing—to the imagination. It wasn't some broad outline of his package—I swore I got detail, and fuck if he wasn't half hard as he struggled to bring those beefy thighs together. I pulled my gaze away from the show he was putting on to find Val watching the same thing I was.

I got up, walked over to Val, and grabbed his arm. "Let's go."

"Why? This is better than porn," he whispered. "I don't care if he's the biggest dick on earth. Oh… and it's possible he's in the running for that honor for real."

"We're going because you're my friend."

"Fine." Val jammed the elevator call button. "But you owe me more of an explanation, Pay-*ton*. I want to know exactly what this guy did to piss you off so badly." Val turned back to watch, leaning against the wall next to the elevator, clearly enjoying the display. When the elevator arrived, I grabbed Val and stepped inside, thankful when the doors slid closed again. "Where are we going?"

"Free weights."

"Good idea. We can spot each other and check out the guys in there. But if one of those big guys asks me for a spot, you're on your own." He licked his lips dramatically on our ride down to the basement. The door slid open to black rubber floors, dark walls, the scent of sweat and testosterone, and the clang of weights dropping to the floor. I wasn't sure this was the best idea I'd ever had, but I went right over to the dumbbells, picked up a pair, and started doing bicep curls.

The man next to me was between sets, and he watched. "Hey, slow down, little dude. You'll get more out of it if you control the weight, like this." He lifted a dumbbell that I'd need both hands to get off the rack and curled it with no problem, slow and easy. "Slow adds resistance and builds the muscle faster."

"Like this?" I asked, and I did it slower. The guy nodded. I watched myself in the mirror. Val came to stand next to me, and he did the same thing, looking over at the gargantuan man like he was a huge meal.

"Thanks," Val told him when he set down the weight. "What's the best way of working the triceps?" The man showed him how to do triceps extensions bent over a weight bench and then proceeded to watch every move Val made. I moved away from their mating dance and found my own place to finish my workout.

Val was having the time of his life playing the "dude-sel" in distress. I half expected the big guy to strip Val down and take him right there. Hell, if the room had been empty, he might have done just that. By the time I was done, I had worked out all my anger at Beckett and felt like a fool for reacting like that in the first place. Val finished about the same time. When we pushed the call button for the elevator, Val's new friend, Rod, decided to join us for the ride up to the locker room floor.

"This is my friend Payton," Val told Rod. "He's new here in New York. Do you live in the area?" Now that he'd done his social duty and made the necessary introductions, Val was all about Rod, or more accurately, getting access to Rod's rod.

In the locker room, Rod just happened to have the locker a few doors down, and he kept watching Val like he was dessert. I let the two of them be, got undressed, slipped on shower shoes, and headed to the shower area with my dark blue towel wrapped tightly around my waist, using it as a shield against whoever might be lurking in the showers. Usually Val and I went in together. It always reminded me of the way ladies went to the bathroom in pairs. Now I understood—it was for protection. As soon as I turned the corner, I saw the guy who was always there, taking eight showers in hopes of catching the eye of someone who might be interested. I went right to the first open shower, not looking at anyone. Once I pulled the curtain closed, I took off the towel and hung it away from the spray before turning on the water. I washed well, but as fast as I could. Plenty of others were showering as well.

Once I was done, I dried off and wrapped the towel around my waist before pushing the curtain aside. I stepped out and saw that the drape on the stall across from me was jammed to the side. Beckett stood in the stall in all his glory, running his hands through his shoulder-length black hair, the definition of strength and power in a package that I couldn't take my eyes off of.

I reminded myself about everything he'd done to me, and my hatred made a reappearance. I took a step toward the locker room and was bumped hard from behind. I went sprawling forward and managed to catch myself on the tile wall so I didn't go flying headfirst onto the floor.

I turned and glared at Beckett, who looked at me, squinting like he was trying to figure something out. "Sorry," he said insincerely. "You should watch where you're going."

"Yeah, me," I called. I grabbed my towel so it didn't end up down around my feet and stalked out to my locker, muttering.

"What was that?" Val asked. He was just now getting ready to go into the shower. Apparently he and Rod had been talking—or maybe making out somewhere, judging by how swollen Val's lips were.

"I said they should shoot the stupid people to put them out of our misery." I yanked open the locker and started getting dressed.

"What happened?"

"Gorilla Boy nearly ran me over and then said I should watch where I was going." I pulled on my underwear and then the old comfortable jeans from my bag. "I wonder if he's capable of watching out for anyone else other than himself, or if he simply feels that he's the center of the universe." I was working myself up good and needed to calm down, so I shut up, turned away, and finished dressing.

"Wait for me," Val said as he went toward the showers.

"Aren't you meeting your friend?" I teased. I was rewarded with one of Val's haughty looks.

"No!" he said louder than necessary, his voice thick with indignation. "I'm not that kind of guy." Val's serious expression lasted about two seconds, and then he broke into a grin. "He's meeting me for dinner at La Maison at seven. Then I think I can be happy tomorrow is Friday and I don't have to go into work until noon."

"Slut," I whispered.

"Prude."

"Bitch."

"Tightass."

"God, I hope so. It has been a while," I countered, breaking the line. Val burst into peals of laughter that made a lot of the other guys look our way. I ignored them. "Go get cleaned up. I'll meet you in the lobby." I gathered my things, placing my dress shirt and tie in my bag along with my good shoes. I draped my suit coat and pants over my arm, grabbed my bag, and left the locker room, grateful not to be knocked off my feet as I avoided Beckett entering my bay of lockers.

The cool thing was that he'd looked at me more than once and didn't seem to recognize me. That was fine, as far as I was concerned. Hell, I hoped he was in town for some gorilla convention or something and I'd never have to lay eyes on him—or get out of his way—again.

Val met me in the lobby a little while later, practically bouncing as he joined me. Yeah, I was jealous, but that was the story of my life. I wasn't cute the way Val was, and I didn't have his sharp wit or ability to talk to anyone. He always seemed to know what to say to everyone to make them like him. My younger brother, Henry, had that same ability, but I never had and never would.

I carefully set my coat and pants over the arm of one of the chairs, put on my coat, and then picked my clothes back up, along with my bag, before following Val outside. The wind had died down, and the city felt just a little warmer.

"Come on, let's go home. We can have a drink or something if you want before I meet Rod for dinner," Val said.

"He actually asked you out?"

"Don't make me hit you. I'm not a slut, and, yeah, he asked me out. I've seen him around, and he said he's seen me. The guy's pretty shy."

"Not that shy. Where did you make out, anyway?" I motioned to his lips, which I had to admit looked a lot less swollen than they had before.

"He kissed me. It was pleasant, and then he asked me out for dinner. Believe it or not, he acted like a gentleman, and it's been a long time since I dated one of those. The guy's huge, but nice."

"Sorry for being snarky," I said as we stopped at a street corner and waited for traffic to part. "I guess I lump all the muscle-headed guys like that in the same bucket—"

"—as Beckett. Yeah, I get that now. See, I could never figure it out. You're a good-looking guy."

"Not like you." The light changed and we crossed the street with a throng of other people.

"What do you mean?" Val asked. "You're cute. You certainly don't look like Pay-*ton* any longer." Val paused and turned. "You have great eyes and a good body. Guys notice you, but you don't see them because you assume most guys act like the gorilla at the gym."

"So you're Freud now?" I countered defensively as we turned down a quiet street and continued walking the couple of blocks to our building.

"Don't have to be. You're my friend, and I always wondered why you were so quiet. You should be more assertive and outgoing. Guys would pick up on that, and you'd be the belle of the ball." He did a little twirl on the sidewalk, and I couldn't help laughing. Val was good for the spirit—at least, he was good for my spirit.

"Come on, Valerina, let's get home before we freeze to death." I picked up the pace, and Val went along with me. We had to stop at the light near our building, and when we finally stepped inside, the warmth felt amazing on my hands and face. "Let me drop my things in the apartment and I'll be right up."

"Sure," Val called as he climbed the stairs. I got out my keys and unlocked the door. As soon as I was inside, I checked that everything was okay. I still wasn't used to living in the city, and watching too many crime shows on TV had left me a little skittish.

The apartment only had basic furniture collected from a few secondhand stores. My one extravagance was the television, but even it wasn't high-end. If anyone did break in, that was about all they would get. There was a bedroom nook, which was merely a small indentation off the single room, separated by a screen. It created the illusion of a bedroom, which was enough for me. But what I really loved about the place was the small courtyard I could access by way of a door in the kitchen area. It was small and surrounded by other buildings, floored with concrete, but I had the only access and there weren't even other windows. So it was like a separate room of my own.

I wandered out there, immediately forgetting I was supposed to go upstairs. I went back inside and pulled open the door when I heard knocking. Val hurried inside.

"I figured you must have gotten distracted." He walked through and out to the courtyard. "You know, this weekend we should find you some chairs, maybe with cushions. I was also thinking if we found a rug to cover this floor it could be nice out here. Maybe some candles and stuff."

"But what do I do with it all during the winter?"

"It isn't that much." Val turned around. "Maybe some plants that like shade."

"Okay, I'll think about it," I agreed and went back inside. "Do you want to have drinks here?"

"No, I have everything set out upstairs," Val told me with an excited smile. "Come on, we'll sit and talk a few minutes before I have to leave." I followed him up after locking the door behind me.

Val's apartment was the lap of luxury compared to mine. Much of the furniture was antique and had been his grandmother's. Val had repainted the walls a light tan and covered the walls in his taste in ultramodern art, but other than that, the apartment was sumptuous with rich fabrics and pillows. It reflected Val's personality perfectly. I sat on the sofa, and Val brought in a silver tray with glasses and a cocktail shaker on it. He poured the light blue concoction and handed me a glass before filling his own. "You owe me more of the story about the gorilla at the gym." He held up his glass, and we clinked.

"You mean Beckett. I'd really prefer not to talk about it. I feel like an idiot for letting some guy who doesn't even remember me get me all worked up like that. He's some big, muscle-bound man with more body than brains." I sipped from the glass and smiled. "So are you planning to bring Rod's rod back here after dinner?"

"Of course not. This is just a first date. What do you take me for?" Val's fake Southern accent was hilarious. "I don't plan on doing anything other than having dinner."

"Uh-huh." I couldn't help myself.

"What?"

"Don't give me that. You're wearing your 'come fuck me' clothes. The jeans are practically poured on, and the shirt is so short I can see skin already."

"You do care."

"Of course I do. If you want to go out and get laid, do it. But don't play this game like you aren't thinking about it. Be honest with yourself." I drank some more. "You said he acted like a gentleman, so you should too. See if he really likes you before you jump in bed with him."

Val got up and went to stand in front of the mirror. "God, you're right." He set down his glass and hurried through the apartment to the bedroom. "I need to change. He was nice, and I'm acting like some club kid who can't keep it in his pants. Well, more than usual." I stayed where I was, and Val came out a few minutes later in nicer slacks and a silk shirt that shimmered.

"Yeah. You look like you care what he thinks, but it doesn't scream, 'Take me home and fuck me.'"

"What does it say?" Val asked as he turned in front of the mirror, trying to see how his ass looked in the pants.

"It says, 'Take me to dinner and we'll see,'" I told him. "And stop trying to see your own butt. You look good." I handed him his glass, and we finished our drinks. "Go on and get ready to go. Meet Rod and have a good time. Be sure to text me when you get home."

"Is that necessary?"

"Of course it is." I walked to the door and pulled it open. "Have fun, but not too much fun. My mom told me once before she passed not to give everything away too quickly. Always leave them wanting more and they'll keep coming back."

"I'm taking relationship advice from the guy who never goes on a date," Val teased. He hugged me. "I'll see you tomorrow."

I left and went downstairs to my apartment, where I ended up spending much of the evening watching TV. Yeah, I was handing out relationship advice while I spent my free time stuck in front of the television. I was really pathetic and needed to get out, have some fun, and find a life of my own.

At about bedtime, I got a text that I thought was from Val, but it turned out it was from my boss. Great. First he'd taken away the account I'd worked for, and now he wanted me to come in early. I went to bed wondering what that was about.

CHAPTER 2—LIVID

THANK GOD for the coffee shop on the way to work; otherwise I never would have made it to the conference room on time. It seemed I was not the last to arrive—an agent named Jane would take that honor—and I took one of two empty seats, as far from the head of the table as I could. We were arranged by a kind of seniority, and the closer to the boss you got, the higher you stood in his estimation. I knew where I stood after the crap the day before, so I took my place and waited for him to come in. Garren sat two seats closer to the head, but at least he had the grace not to gloat. Everyone looked around the table, silently wondering what was up.

Then it hit me. I *was* the last to arrive. The empty chair on the other side of the table represented the one person who wasn't coming. The conference room door opened, and the head of the agency strode in. Claude Maxim was everything his name would suggest. He was a presence in every room he entered. You couldn't help looking at him, with his stunning blue eyes, aquiline nose, and perfectly coiffed snow-white hair. He wasn't more than forty-five, and he looked like he'd soaked up moonlight—a gorgeous man, for sure.

"All right. We have a huge day ahead of us. As some of you might have guessed, Jane is no longer with the firm. Her prospects haven't panned out, and she has decided to pursue another line of work. I suspect she'll be selling Mary Kay out of her car."

A snicker went around the table. Claude thought he was funny, and since he was the head of the firm, he was, regardless.

"I can sift through her clients and see what's viable," Garren offered.

"No. You're busy enough," Claude answered. His gaze scanned the table. "But your point is taken. We'll need to go through her dog pile and see if there are any gems in it. I've begun the process, and I

17

expect that you'll all provide any help needed." I felt Claude's gaze fall on me, and I stopped myself from fidgeting in the chair. "Are there any questions?" Claude waited, but there were none, so he left the room, and the agency employees started filing out behind him.

To my surprise, Gloria, one of the senior agents, stayed behind, got up from her seat next to Claude, and walked down to my end of the table. I was about to get up, but she slid into the chair next to mine.

"I heard about what happened yesterday," she said.

"Yeah." What else could I say?

"It happens to all of us. In my opinion, Garren should have let you have him. You were the one who did the work. But sometimes that's not how it goes. In this business you can't expect star talent to fall in your lap. You need to look for the new talent and build them up. It can take a long time. That's what happened with Kyle Weathers." I knew he was her biggest client, one who'd made the transition from Broadway to Hollywood. "He had talent but no direction when I found him in a little theater in Brooklyn. He and I worked together to build his career into the mega sensation it is. You'll do the same. You just need to find them." She patted my hand. The scent of cigarettes mixed with perfume permeated my nose. "And I know you will. You have a talent for this business. So don't let one setback bother you." She stood up and walked toward the door, flashing me a half smile before leaving the room. Since I wouldn't get anything done sitting here, I went to my tiny office, where I began formulating a plan of action.

"Claude would like to see you in his office," Millie said as she passed with an armload of files. She was Claude's overworked assistant.

I stood and relieved her of the files, carrying them to her desk. Then I knocked on Claude's door before going inside. The one thing that always surprised me about Claude's office was that it wasn't much bigger than mine, just much more richly appointed, with two sculptures on the credenza behind him and lighted abstract paintings on the walls.

"Close the door," he said without looking up. I did as he asked. "Since things didn't go your way yesterday, I've decided to give you an opportunity." He lifted a small stack of files from his desk, and I stepped forward to take them. "These are the clients of Jane's that we will be transitioning to you. I have already asked Millie to notify them, and you can arrange to meet with each of them over the next few days to get acquainted." Claude caught my gaze. "Now these," he said as he handed me another small stack, "are the few people from Jane's dog pile that I believe are worth pursuing further. Those are working actors." He pointed to the first stack. "These are people with potential. The remainders are in the Seussian stack that Millie will send letters to. Like I said, these are your challenge, especially the one on top. He has real potential. Jane saw him in"—Claude wiggled his fingers in the air—"something and said he was good. Reminded her of Schwarzenegger. If it's too much, you can ask Garren for help."

That guaranteed I would do whatever it took, because he knew I would never again give Garren another chance at anything that was mine.

"Thank you." I looked at the folders I held in my hands. I wasn't sure what else to say. Claude had already turned his attention back to his desk, so I left the office, closing the door behind me. I passed Millie's desk—she was already sifting through the pile of files so she could send out the "we're sorry" letters. The woman never stopped working.

I hurried to my office and closed the door. I looked over the call list for my new clients. I'd have to call each one and set up appointments. Then I picked up the file for the guy Claude had shown an interest in. I opened it and a head shot and then a name screamed out at me: Beckett Huntington. "Son of a bitch!" I groaned, grateful the door was closed.

I was tempted to throw the file across the room. I mean, fucking hell, it seemed I couldn't get away from him, even though I'd moved halfway across the country. I was not going to take on that asshole as a client. This was my life and my chance to make something of myself, and Beckett Huntington was not going to be a part of it. Hell, maybe I could pass the file on to Garren. Of course that would also mean Claude would know, and I'd be in a world of hurt. He had given me the file, after all. I smiled and set the file aside. Maybe Mr. Huntington could just sit in my file drawer and rot. The bastard had made my life hell for months. I sure as shit wasn't going to do a damn thing to help him.

My phone rang and I answered it.

"You were gone early," Val chirped.

"And you got in very late. So much for that 'I'm not a slut' crap."

Val snorted. "We stayed out, talked, lost track of time, and I got back just after midnight, thank you very much." There was a definite dreamy quality to Val's voice. "He was really nice."

"Are you going to see him again?" I asked, playing naïve.

"We have a date for a week from Saturday. This weekend he's competing, and I have to work second shift at the IT help desk during the week, but he already asked me out and said he would call me during the week just to hear my voice." I suspected Val was dancing around his apartment like a ballerina at that very moment. I could almost see him. "What did you get up to?"

"Nothing much. I had to be in the office early. I got some new clients from Claude this morning, along with some prospects. And guess who's at the top of the prospect list? Think gorilla."

"No way!" His voice was so loud I had to move the phone from my ear. "That thing can act… well, something other than dumb?" He cackled, and I laughed along with him. "What are you going to do?"

"I don't know. I was so angry when I saw the file I nearly tore it to shreds." Hell, I still wanted to. I reached for it, fighting the impulse to turn the fucking thing into confetti. "The last thing I want is to be anywhere near that piece of shit." I kept my voice down, but I wanted to scream. I waited for Val to say something, but he was quiet. "What?"

"Don't cut off your face to spite your nose, or however that saying goes. Do you think he recognized you?"

"I doubt it. There was almost nothing behind his eyes at all. I think his brains might have liquefied at some point. When I saw the file, I swear I had smoke coming out of my ears."

"Okay. Calm down and think. You have a job to do, and you're a good guy. Unlike me. I could throw him in the trash easy, but you'd always wonder if you did something wrong. So meet with him. If he has real talent, then make yourself a boatload of money off him. If he doesn't, get his hopes up and then dash them so you can watch him fold like a house of cards." Val laughed like the Grinch. "Either way, you win."

"Remind me never to get on your bad side." I chuckled, feeling a little better. "I need to go."

"Tell me all about it when I see you." After Val hung up, I made calls to each of the current clients to introduce myself and set up times to meet. Then I started on the prospective clients, asking each actor to come into the office so we could meet face-to-face. My appointment book filled quickly. Granted, they were only initial meetings, and the hard work would be arranging for auditions, but I had to take this first step.

I put off calling Beckett until last. I half hoped the call would go to voice mail—then I could just leave a message and pray he didn't call me back.

"Yeah."

"Is this Beckett Huntington?" I said, lowering my voice slightly. Why, I had no idea.

"Yeah, who is this?"

"I'm Pay Gowan with the Maxim Agency. I was calling because of your interest in representation." I hoped like hell my name didn't ring any bells with him. In school everyone called me Payton, so I figured I was pretty safe.

"What about Jane?" he asked. "I talked to her a few weeks ago, and she said she expected to be able to represent me."

"Jane has decided to make a career change," I told him.

"Shit," he groaned. I took a little pleasure in his disappointment. Let him wonder and worry. He'd made me feel uncomfortable and stripped away my self-confidence too many times. He could experience a setback for once. "So what do I have to do now?"

"I'd like to meet you, find out what you can do. Maybe see you in action. When can you come into the office to meet with me?" I wanted to blow the asshole off, but this was my job and I needed to be professional.

"You'll need to come prepared to show me what you can do." I'd put him through his paces and then stomp on his dreams. Of course I threw that idea aside because helping him would help me as well. On top of that, if I didn't do my best, then Claude would give Garren his shot, and that galled me almost as much as the thought of working with Beckett.

"I can do that." He sounded excited. "Just tell me what sort of reading you'd like."

"No reading." I wasn't going to make this easy on him. "I want something from memory, fully acted and prepared. Maybe something from Curly in *Oklahoma*." I threw that last part in because I couldn't resist it. "Can you be here at three today?" I knew I was pushing it, but it felt good to be the one in control.

"I have to work until…. Yes. I'll be there." His excitement ramped up. I ended the call, adding him to my schedule. I was taking way too much delight in this.

I ate lunch in my office and spent the afternoon in meetings. Things moved very quickly for the rest of the day, and by three I had met with two of my new clients and with Gloria, who had contacts in every production company in town. She made a few introductions for me and helped arrange some auditions.

"I appreciate the help," I told her.

"Don't thank me yet. They haven't got the parts, but you're doing me a favor as well. Whenever we can supply good candidates for a wide range of parts, it makes the firm more valuable, and that helps us all. Now go and make sure your clients are prepped and ready, and for God's sake they had better show up on time."

They would if I had to take them there myself. I hurried back to my office and made some calls. I could tell my new clients were impressed, and they promised to be at their auditions on time and ready to go. I made notes in my calendar to call them a few hours before as a reminder. It was a good day.

My phone rang. "Yes," I said.

"Pay, there's a huge man waiting out in the lobby for you," Millie said with a touch of trepidation. "He says he's here for a meeting, but…."

"It's okay. I think he's my three o'clock."

"I'll escort him back, then." She hung up and I stood behind my desk. I was going to meet this man again formally from a position of strength.

Millie knocked on my door, then opened it, smiling a little before stepping back. Beckett Huntington stepped into my office, and his eyes immediately widened. I heard him gasp softly.

"Thank you, Millie," I said, motioning for him to sit. She left the door open.

Beckett stood just inside the office. I waited to see what he would do.

"You're the guy…."

"Yes. Yesterday at the gym."

"You ran into—"

I cleared my throat.

"I ran into you," he clarified.

I nodded. "And…." I prompted, enjoying his discomfort immensely.

"Maybe I should go." He shifted from foot to foot and pulled at his collar.

"If that's what you'd like. But this chance isn't going to come around again." Why I didn't let him go was beyond me. Maybe it was the scared insecurity in his blue eyes. "Now, think about the way you acted yesterday. You were rude and almost pushed me off my machine when all I wanted was to get a drink, and you practically ran me over and acted as though it was my fault, when the one who wasn't looking where he was going was you." I motioned again to the chair and then sat down myself. "What if you were my client, and I had arranged an audition for you, and the man you treated that way was the producer or director? You never know who anyone is in this town."

Beckett swallowed. "I understand," he said softly. So far he seemed to have only equated me with the guy from the gym, which was fine. It felt strange to have him in my office, but it also gave me a sense of authority since he obviously didn't remember me.

"In this business, you get one chance—if any at all—and to waste it on something…." I sat back and let my words settle in… for him and for me. I was going to take my own advice, keep my mouth shut, and do my job. "Do you have photos?"

He nodded and pulled some glossies out of his bag. "Jane told me what I should have taken."

I looked through them, then set them on my desk. "The head shots are fine, and we can use some of the others, but not these." I handed some back.

"Those are the ones I really like," he protested.

They were the real muscle shots. "I understand. You've worked years on your body, but the thing is, there are only so many parts for guys who look like the Hulk, and they only make so many Hercules movies. The Met only puts on *Tristan und Isolde* once a decade, where they need rowers." I let that hang in the air for a few seconds, then stood. "I booked a conference room, and we're going to go in there. You can do what you've prepared, and then I'm going to have you read something blind for me. Then I'll make a decision."

I stood and grabbed my file before leading him to the conference room and closing the door. I sat down and motioned him to the front. "Go."

I watched Beckett squirm a little, then he turned and began. The scene from *Death of a Salesman* lasted only a few minutes, but I was drawn to Beckett's Willy Loman. When he was done, I wanted to know more. Not that Beckett would ever play this character, but to see a guy as huge as he was read a character who came off as small and desperate and make it believable was more than I had been expecting.

"You wanted something from *Oklahoma*," Beckett said.

"I was teasing," I told him. I handed Beckett the scene I wanted him to read, gave him a few minutes to prepare, then asked him to do the monologue.

To my surprise he did very well. The prepared piece he should have nailed, and he did, but he even brought depth to the piece I'd grabbed from a pile of scripts. It was nothing, but he made the work sound amazing.

24

"Okay," I said, stopping him. "I think I've seen enough." God, I had been prepared for him to suck so I could send him on his way, but that wasn't the case at all.

"Was it good?" Beckett asked.

"Yes. Now we need to get you looking like you're serious." I motioned him to the table. "I want you to get some new pictures taken. We'll keep the ones you have in case a Conan-esque film comes up, but you can be more than that. I want you to soften yourself. You have a real talent, but with the look you have now, very few roles will come your way. Do you have a tuxedo?" Beckett shook his head. "Then rent one and have pictures taken in it. Show you can be dashing, and get a plain sweater—I want you to put together a college look. We know from looking at you that you could play football players, but let's make you look like other kinds of athletes. It's all about perception and what you can pull off. I think a few with glasses would be interesting. Otherwise, people are going to look at you and not see beyond your size. I want to showcase that you are more than that." I rolled my eyes and slid a piece of paper and a pen across the table. "Also, never go anywhere without a pen and something to write on. It isn't necessary to take notes while you're there, but jot down important details as soon as you leave."

"Okay." He began writing down what I'd told him.

"If you agree, I'll have a representation contract drawn up, and then once the pictures are done, we'll start the audition process."

Beckett jumped to his feet, and for a few seconds he looked like a huge puppy. "I've been living on a friend's couch for weeks, and I was about to give up and go home."

"There is still plenty of hard work ahead. Never forget that." I handed him my business card and verified that the information I had for him was correct. "Do you know a photographer?"

"Jane arranged for the last one."

"I'll arrange for this one, and we'll get you set up. But I need to stress this: I don't want you getting bigger, and the vascularity isn't attractive away from competition. Do you understand?"

"Yeah."

"Good. Now hone your craft and treat every audition as though it's the part of your life." I stood and put out my hand.

"I appreciate this. I won't let you down." Beckett shook my hand firmly. "I'm grateful you're not letting what happened yesterday affect things."

I nodded. My mouth went dry as he held my hand. I blinked a few times, then pulled away as a tingle of excitement zipped up my back. No way in hell was I going to allow anything like that. I backed up in the hope of hiding the flush burning in my face. Where the hell had that come from? I was not attracted to Beckett Huntington. *Not happening.* "I'll call you as soon as the paperwork is ready and when I have the appointment set up with the photographer." Beckett stared at the floor. "What is it?"

"I don't know anything about tuxedos and stuff like that."

"Do you have friends who do?"

Beckett shook his head. "My friends know about jeans and gym shorts. I spent the last few years as a competitive bodybuilder, but I've wanted to act since I fell into it in high school." I closed my eyes and let the anger that welled up cool back down. Showing anger wouldn't be productive. I needed to keep my head.

"All right. I'll make arrangements for that as well." Gloria told me once that sometimes agents needed to be babysitters and even wardrobe consultants. Looked like this was one of those times. "I'll go with you to the photographer as well. Just make sure you get the paperwork back to me right away so we can get you working."

"I will." He smiled brightly. "Thank you so much." He hurried toward the door, and I followed him out and led him back to the lobby.

"Was that your latest client?" Garren asked from behind me once the elevator doors had closed. "What are you going to get him cast for?"

"He can act, he looks amazingly hot, and I'm sure I can turn him into a heartthrob." I turned and smiled at Garren.

"I wouldn't have bothered."

"He didn't read for you," I said without heat. Then I turned and went back to my office. I had calls to make and enough appointments to keep me busy the rest of the day.

BY THE time I got home, I was exhausted and exhilarated. I was also so pissed off I wanted to stomp myself into the concrete. Instead of going to my apartment, I went right up to Val's and knocked, but he wasn't home. I returned to my apartment and remembered I should have stopped for something to eat. I already knew there was nothing in the house, so I went right back out and down to the corner market. I got a light dinner and took it back, wishing I had someone to talk to. I sat in my chair and ate, watching nothing on television. Once I'd eaten, I put the trash away, then pulled out my phone, and called my dad.

"Hey, son," he answered. "I was wondering if you were all right there in the big city."

"I'm fine, Dad. How are all the students?" My father was a grounds supervisor for Central Michigan University. His job was the reason I was able to go to college: the university gave family members of employees a break on tuition.

"The usual. Last night they strung toilet paper over half the trees on campus, so we were cleaning up that mess for hours."

I laughed, because it happened every year. "Some things never change," I said softly.

"How are things? Do you need anything?"

"Just to talk. Things are going well. I got my own clients today, and I think I signed a new talent."

"You don't sound sure."

"I'm sure about his talent, but there's some other crap that's thrown me." I sighed, deciding just to get it out there. "The client is Beckett Huntington."

Dad went quiet for a while. "I remember that kid. The hoodlum." My dad had understood and done what he could at the time, but I didn't tell him half the things that had gone on. I didn't want him to be ashamed of me or think I was a wuss or something. It was bad enough that I was gay, and I wanted him to be proud of me. "What's he done?"

"He's my latest client," I confessed. "He doesn't remember me from school."

"Why would you do that? Take him on as a client?"

"Because he was really good, Dad. He has talent, a real gift." I felt as though I was going to cry, but I held it in. This so wasn't fair.

"What are you really upset about?" he asked, Dad always seemed to know exactly what questions to ask. "I take it he isn't the same person he was back then, any more than you are."

"No. I guess he isn't, but… why couldn't I have that talent? I wanted it so bad, and I worked for it. I studied and learned my lines. No, that's not right. I learned everyone's lines. I read them all and worked at each part, but he took it all away."

"I can't begin to understand what you mean." Dad sounded so tired that I felt guilty for laying all this crap at his feet. He didn't deserve it, and everything I was talking about had happened years earlier. It was over and in the past, but I was acting like it was yesterday. "The only answer I can give you is that talent is something we're born with, not something we can learn. We can hone it, make the gifts we're given sharper and better, but we can't create them out of nothing."

"But I tried so hard."

"Payton, you always did your best at everything you tried."

"But…."

"Look, when I was about twelve, your grandmother decided I should play the piano because she loved Liberace and thought if I learned to play, I could be like him and make a lot of money, play at parties, you get the picture. I liked it. Playing the piano was something I really liked, and I used to practice every afternoon. Until Mom stopped the lessons."

"Why?"

"Because I was all thumbs and couldn't hit the right notes to save my life. I liked playing, but I stunk… bad. And apparently my dad threatened to leave home if she didn't make me stop playing." Dad laughed deeply. "It turns out I'm largely tone-deaf, which came in handy whenever your mother was on the warpath."

"Okay…."

"So we don't get to choose our talents. I found out later that mine was making things grow, and maybe yours isn't acting, the way you once hoped it was, but you have other things you're good at. Just don't let jealousy over what you don't have stand in the way of the things you do best."

"I'll try, Dad."

"Good. And as far as this Beckett kid goes, just do your best for him. See, it's a real talent to be able to see the gifts others have." Dad yawned, and I checked the clock. "I got to go to bed because I'm working the early shift."

"All right. Thanks for listening."

"Anytime. You know that."

We said good night, and as I ended the call, I heard footsteps on the stairs outside the door. I pulled it open and saw Val heading up.

"Did you skewer him?" Val asked, coming back down and over to the door. I stepped back and he came inside. I didn't like to have company at my place. It was too sparse and unwelcoming. I really needed to get decent furniture.

"No. I signed him." I sighed, knowing I was a fool. "Now he's my client, and it's my job to make sure he has the best career possible. I'll get him auditions and watch him get parts I'll never be able to play. Hell, I'll even have to dress him and probably go to the damn auditions with him." I closed the door with more force than necessary.

"I don't get you. Why didn't you let someone else take him as a client?"

"Because he's really good." That was the only explanation that I could allow myself to vocalize. There was no way I could tell Val that when Beckett was performing his scene, I was completely transfixed by his lips, or how expressive his cobalt eyes were. Even the way he cocked his eyebrows at just the right moment was perfect. "The guy is huge, okay? But I believed him as Willy Loman, and he did a great job on the blind reading too. I was really impressed, and that kind of talent isn't something you let get away in this business. If you do, then someone else, like Garren, will be waiting in the wings."

"So you did the right thing and signed him regardless of how it made you feel." Val put an arm around my shoulder. "Let's go up to my place and have a drink or three."

"You too?"

"Yeah. It sounds like the day was crap all around."

I grabbed my keys and locked the door, then followed Val upstairs. He let me in, and I sat on his sofa while he got the things together for martinis. Val's were notorious. He waved the vermouth bottle over the glasses and then poured in the gin. They were martinis only in the sense that they were served in martini glasses and had an olive in them.

"So what happened?" I asked.

"I spent an hour on the phone trying to help this guy install his software. He was so stupid. I asked him the kind of computer he had, and he takes a second and tells me it's black."

"No way," I said, laughing.

"Yes. I asked him for the brand name, and he says he doesn't know. I asked what it said on the bottom of the frame of the display. He said there was nothing, so I asked him where he got it, and he said he bought it off a guy on the corner. And then he proceeds to ask me why he'd turned it on but none of the lights came on and the screen didn't light up." Val gulped from his glass and let his head rest on the back of the sofa. "I swear I get every crazy person on earth."

"What did you tell him?"

"I asked if the power cord was plugged in."

"Oh God, let me guess…."

"What power cord?" we said in unison. I broke out laughing and nearly spilled my drink but managed to hold on to it.

"It seems he bought this laptop off a guy on the street for twenty bucks. Lo and behold his neighbor had a power cord that fit, and believe it or not, the computer actually booted up. Of course it had someone else's files on it because it had either been stolen or was just chucked in a dumpster. I told him how to erase the old files, then walked him through updating everything. By the time we hung up, I was frazzled to hell, but the guy was happy and thanking me no end.

Of course, all that will come crashing down when his neighbor wants his power cord back." Val drained his glass and refilled it. "Thank God there's just one more day in this sucky week."

"Was that the worst thing that happened?"

"No. It was just the funniest. I thought once I was through with college I would be changing the world—developing great software and making everyone's lives better. Instead, I'm resurrecting boat anchors and getting street-corner computers going again."

"I thought you liked your job."

"I do. But I don't want to get stuck doing this the rest of my life," he whined.

"You won't. And if you want to change the world, then do it on your own. You'll never do it working for someone else. Jobs and Wozniak didn't do that, and neither did Bill Gates or that guy who started Oracle."

"Ellison," Val supplied, but I continued because I was on a roll.

"Yeah, him. So come up with your own great idea and go with it. But if you become a dick like that Facebook guy, I'll smack you upside the head." I smiled and sipped from my glass, the gin biting as it slid down my throat. "You have extra time—think of something and make it work. You live in New York, where lots of things can happen, and you're surrounded by people who know more people, so all you need is the great idea and the ability to sell it. And you can do both." I drained my glass and groaned. My father was right: I could see the talent in others.

"You should be a motivational speaker," Val quipped, and it took all my restraint not to smack him.

"Yeah, like Pinocchio in that commercial." I rolled my eyes. "Look, if you hit it big, you have to promise to remember me."

"Of course I will," Val said, raising his voice to sound like a Southern belle. "I promise to remember all the little people who made this possible." He sounded like he was making an Oscar acceptance speech, and then he burst out laughing. "Come on, how about another drink?" He refilled our glasses. "Everything seems better when seen through the bottom of a glass."

I did feel better, and a little toasted, and I had to be careful I didn't tumble down the stairs when it was time to go.

"There's just one more thing I want to know," Val said, rolling slightly on his heels. He'd insisted on walking me home, which consisted of one flight of stairs. "Are you really upset about what this Beckett guy did to you in high school? Or are you all up in arms because you have the hots for him?"

"Where did that come from?" I demanded. Sometimes he saw way more than I wanted him to.

"Don't get your panties in a twist, but I saw the way you were looking at him." Val giggled as I unlocked my door, said good night, and went inside. I checked through the peephole to make sure he made it back upstairs before getting ready for bed.

CHAPTER 3—LONGING

SATURDAY, LATE in the morning, I was wondering how I'd let Val drag me out to a bar the night before. In his words, it was "because it's time you got out and met people," but the only people I could remember the next morning were Mr. Vodka and Mrs. Rum—a couple who were not a match made in heaven. By the time I got up and out of the bathroom, Val was already pounding on my door.

He bounced in, telling me to get up, we were going outside. "It's a wonderful day, so let's go down to the park."

I groaned but couldn't come up with an argument against it, other than the fact that it was all the way downtown. Val was determined, so we spent the afternoon wandering the park and tossing a Frisbee he'd shoved in the backpack he'd brought along. Of course, Val caught the eyes of half a dozen guys while we were there. I swore he collected phone numbers the way guys used to collect stamps. I wondered if he had an album he pasted them into so someday when he was old, he could look at them, sigh wistfully, and remember what it felt like to be young… and horny.

We stopped at a bodega on the way home and got dinner. Val had worn me out, but he still insisted on having drinks.

"How about a Diet Coke each and we can watch a movie?" I asked.

"*The Hobbit?*" Val asked hopefully. I had no idea why he loved those Hobbit movies so much, but I acquiesced, and we spent the next few hours devouring a huge bowl of popcorn on Val's couch. I dozed off before the end, but Val nudged me awake in time for the dragon parts, which I liked, and then I went home, dragging my butt to bed.

Sunday I slept in and had the most amazing time doing laundry and spending a whole hour cleaning the apartment. I did get out to do some shopping and found a cool metal chair from the fifties for the patio. I hauled it home and set it out there. It looked lonely, but it would do for now. I decided I needed to get some Rust-Oleum to paint it, but that could wait until I stopped at the hardware store during the week.

Monday morning was the weekly agency meeting, and I sat in my usual place. Just before the start of the meeting, Gloria got up from her seat and walked down the table. "You sit there," she told me, motioning toward Jane's empty chair. I got up and sat across from Garren, just as Claude came in to start the meeting. I expected looks or grief from the others, but no one said anything. Apparently I'd made Claude happy.

"I don't understand," I told Gloria once the meeting was over.

"You will," she said with a smile before she left the conference room. I found out later in the day that two of the clients I'd sent to auditions got their parts, and that I'd helped Gloria land a huge part for one of her clients. How that worked I had no idea, but then, when it came to Broadway, sometimes the politics could be more powerful than anything else.

I spent the morning making calls and answered one just before lunch.

"Payton, it's Giles Winter. I have an opening at ten o'clock tomorrow for your client if you can get him here." Beckett had returned the contract, and I had been trying to get him in for his pictures, but the photographers were booked solid.

"That's great. Give me ten minutes and I'll call you back and confirm."

I hung up and called Beckett. "I have a photography appointment for you tomorrow at ten."

"That's fast."

"We have to take advantage of it or it could be weeks. Can you be ready?"

"I need to get a tuxedo."

"Okay. Get to my office as soon as you can. I'll make a few calls to see where we can go to get what we need." I hung up and called Marvin, Gloria's assistant. He was one of those guys who had the town wired, and he told me where I could get a tuxedo in any size on short notice. When Beckett arrived, I met him in the lobby. We rode the elevator down to the street and hailed a cab.

"You have all the other things you need?" I asked once I'd given the driver the address and we'd pulled out into traffic.

"Yeah. I asked a friend, and she helped me pick out some things that would soften the way I look." He didn't sound happy about it.

"I know you worked hard, but it's important that you have an image that's versatile. Trust me, everyone will see that you're handsome and hot. But they need to see you as vulnerable and intelligent too, even dashing."

"You think I'm hot?" Beckett asked.

"That's what you got out of that?" I countered, rolling my eyes. I was certainly not having a conversation about his hotness, which was off the charts, but going there was not an option. He was sex on a stick, and in that enclosed space, his scent, mixed with soap and even a touch of lavender, turned the cab into a libido-building caldron of pheromones that went straight my head. I sat as close to the door as I could, trying to breathe through my mouth so I could think clearly. I turned to him and saw him looking back, mouth open a little, wetting his lips slightly with his tongue. He turned away when he saw me looking, and I watched out the window as we made the final turn and approached our destination.

I placed my bag over my lap and breathed as normally as I could, sighing to myself when we pulled over to the curb. Beckett got out, and with relief, I paid the driver, got a receipt, and led Beckett inside the formalwear store.

They had an amazing selection, judging by the racks that lined the walls.

"Can I help you?" a gray-haired gentleman in a crisp suit asked as he came around the counter.

"Beckett here has a photo session tomorrow, and we need some images of him in a tuxedo. We'd like to rent one. It should be plain black with a black tie. Make him look like James Bond."

"My," the man said, looking Beckett over like he was lunch, "that's going to be difficult, but if he were playing James Bond, I'd be sure to go see it." He pulled out jackets for Beckett to try on and quickly found one that fit. Then he stared at Beckett, lightly scratching his chin. "I have pants that will fit him around the waist, but I have to go bigger because of his legs." He handed Beckett a pair of pants and pointed toward a fitting room, and Beckett went inside.

When he came out, he looked as though he'd been poured into the pants. They gripped his legs and hips tightly and would probably rip if he flexed. "Those are way too tight," I said, and George, who had introduced himself while we waited, agreed.

"I might have a pair that will work," George said. "Go ahead and take those off. I'll be right back." He walked through a curtain at the back of the shop, and Beckett returned to the dressing room. George came back out a few minutes later with a pair of pants over his arm. "I had a gentleman built like this a year ago. He ordered a custom pair of pants but never picked them up. I've had them all this time. At least someone might get some use out of them." He handed them to me, and I took them inside the dressing area.

Beckett stood behind a curtain. He turned and peered over the rod. I handed him the pants, and he smiled and turned away.

"Come out when you're ready," I said.

"Okay, but bigger pants are only going to be baggier around the waist. I have this problem all the time. I can only wear certain brands of jeans and pants."

"Just try them on," I said.

Beckett came out a minute later holding his shirt up so we could see the pants. They were a little too long, but fit him perfectly otherwise.

"Wow," I said.

"Yeah. These feel nice," Beckett said.

"Good," George said. "Now I'll find you a shirt and you can try on the whole package." George looked through the rack, then handed me a white shirt with a tab collar. I passed it to Beckett, who returned to the dressing room. He stepped out again, shirt open, looking confused.

"There are extra holes and things. What do I do with those?"

Damn, he was stunning, with his open shirt revealing warm, rich skin. "Those are for the shirt studs." I buttoned the shirt for him and had Beckett lift his chin. George handed me a black tie that I fastened around his neck. "Tuck in the tail, and we'll take a look." I stepped back while he did as I asked.

"Is this right?"

"No," I said, chuckling, and I proceeded to straighten the shirt. Beckett was as hard as granite, and damn if I didn't want to see what all that muscle would feel like under my hands. But I kept my thoughts and attention on the task at hand and got everything the way it should be. Then George handed me the jacket and I gave it to Beckett, who slipped it over his shoulders.

"My God," George whispered.

"You can say that again," I agreed. Beckett was stunning—all wide shoulders, narrow waist, and elegant lines. The entire package would look amazing on a red carpet, a stage, or the big screen. "All right," I said, swallowing hard. I had to pull my gaze away from him. "Take a look at yourself in the mirror."

"What size shoes do you wear?" George asked.

"Thirteen," Beckett answered.

George hurried away.

"Isn't this a bit much?" Beckett asked.

"No. The black smooths you out." I moved closer. "See how elegantly you taper from your shoulders down to your waist and then your legs? You look like a statue. Most really big guys look like a huge man who's been stuffed into a tuxedo. You were made to wear these clothes. And when the casting directors see these pictures, they'll see you in the clothes they need you to wear for the film."

"I still don't understand."

"It's simple. Do you want to spend your entire career running around in a loincloth?" I asked, hands on my hips.

"No."

"Then we have to show them you look stunning in fine clothes or that's all you'll get to do. Remember, Arnold spent years as Conan, wearing next to nothing and saying even less. Then he played a killer robot. He was a body. I want more than that for you."

George returned, handed Beckett the shoes, and he slipped them on.

"We'll take it," I said.

"I can give you a good deal on the clothes if you want to buy them. The pants are his"—George waved his hand dismissively—"because they fit and were already paid for. I'm glad to get them out of my back room. The coat and shirt will come to less than forty dollars more than the rental if you buy them."

I handed him my credit card. "Add some studs and cuff links." I'd charge them to the agency. I had a small expense account, and I'd slip the total onto that. *I haven't eaten lunch out for a while.* George put a basic set on the bill. Then he marked the length of Beckett's pants, and Beckett went to put on his regular clothes.

"You should definitely wear more black," I told Beckett when he came back out. "You look stunning in it. It isn't necessary to go extreme. But some nice black shirts with darker pants would look very good on you. If we're sending you to an audition where they want a big man, we'll get you a patterned shirt, though. It will make you look huge."

"Why are you so worried about things like this?" Beckett asked. He handed over the clothes, and George went into the back to hem the pants.

"Because I know you can act. There's no doubt about it. But in an industry where tall, slim, and attractive are very in, you're different. I want to make sure that difference is used to our advantage. You could have a decent career as an actor in historical or adventure movies where the hero is larger than life, but don't you want more?"

"Yes."

"Then let me do my job," I insisted. "Looks are everything, so if you go into an audition looking stunning, they won't be as quick to dismiss you."

"But…."

"You've been to cattle calls, right? Hundreds of people show up, and the producers give you ten seconds. Do you think they do much more than look in those first few seconds? I want them to remember you. If they're gay, I want them hard, and if they're female, wet." I knew I was being crass, but if it got my point across, so be it.

"And if they're straight?"

"I want them to wish they were you, and we do that with clothes."

"Okay." Beckett put his hands up in surrender. "I'll listen to you."

"Good." Otherwise we were both up a creek. Because like it or not, my career advancement was now tied to Beckett's. I had to make him a success or it was likely I'd end up as the next Jane, out on my ear.

Beckett's gaze hardened, and I coughed slightly. "I'll always do my best for you." At least as far as his career was concerned. God, I needed to watch my mouth and keep my eyes off the way he filled out that damned shirt, to the point where it strained across his body. "Your appointment with the photographer is at ten tomorrow." I reached into my bag and pulled out a card with the address on it. "Get there a few minutes early, and I'll help you with the tuxedo if you wish."

Beckett appeared relieved at that. When George returned with the clothes bag, Beckett took it, and we both thanked George. "Come back again anytime," George said as we reached the door. Beckett pulled it open, and we stepped out onto the sidewalk.

Fresh air—I needed it to clear my head. "I'm going to go back to my office. Are you able to get home?" I hailed a cab and it pulled up to the curb. "If not, I'll drop you and then go on." He got in, and I groaned under my breath and followed him inside. He gave the driver his address, which turned out to be just a few blocks from mine. After we dropped him off, I directed the cab back to the office.

"How was the babysitting?" Millie asked with a slight grin when I walked in.

"He's quite a baby," I retorted.

Millie laughed. "Is he really?"

"No. He just needed some help with clothes for a session with a photographer."

"He isn't a model, you know. He's an actor," Claude said from his office doorway.

I felt like a fool. "I wanted to make sure he could show the versatility of his look. Otherwise...."

Claude nodded thoughtfully. "Good thinking." He went back into his office and closed the door. Millie shrugged and I turned, heading back to my office with a smile.

THE FOLLOWING morning, after making all my calls to remind my charges about auditions, I met Beckett at Giles's studio. He was with another client, but his receptionist pointed toward the screen where Beckett could change. "Start with the tuxedo," I told him. "It takes the longest to change into."

"Okay." Beckett carried his clothes behind the screen while I pulled out my phone to check and return messages. The receptionist nearly swallowed her tongue when Beckett stepped back out with his shirt open, the package of studs in his hand.

"Jesus," she whispered under her breath, and all I could do was nod. My mouth was Sahara dry as I stepped closer and helped him with his shirt. Every now and then, my fingers brushed against the smooth, soft skin of his belly or chest. He was warm, and he appeared as immovable as the proverbial brick wall he seemed to be made of. Once I had the studs done, I helped him with the collar, tie, and cuff links. The assistant watched, completely enraptured. Then I held Beckett's jacket for him and stepped out of the way so he could see how he looked in the mirror.

"Fantastic," Giles breathed as he came in. He was tall and olive-skinned, with a slim, artfully trimmed beard. "Come with me and we'll get started." I stepped out of the way and let Beckett follow Giles as they got acquainted.

"We need as many looks as possible," I explained once Giles began setting up the lighting and plain backgrounds.

"This one looks good to me," Giles purred.

I wanted to smack him and step between him and Beckett. Then I wondered where that thought had come from. Beckett was my client, nothing more. He was out of reach for me. I couldn't allow myself to have any feelings for him, not after what had happened in high school. This had to be a professional relationship. That was the only way I could ever deal with him. It kept me in control and him at arm's length. But what amazed me was that Beckett simply looked at me with that gentle half smile he had and ignored Giles for a brief second.

"Okay, let's get you over here," Giles said.

Beckett walked over to the backdrop, and Giles positioned him, checked lighting, and started taking pictures. Beckett wasn't uncomfortable, but he seemed stiff. He took direction, but his eyes were lifeless. "Pretend you're Willy Loman," I told him from off to the side. "Give us that fire." And he did. Almost instantly his jaw set and his eyes blazed. Beckett wasn't a model, but his eyes did convey emotion. After a few minutes, Beckett was sent off to change clothes, and Giles walked over to me.

"What's going on with you two?" he asked. I widened my eyes in surprise. "He watches you instead of me. Even when we're in the height of the session, he knows where you are."

"I'm his new agent, and I think he wants to impress me."

"He certainly isn't interested in impressing me," Giles retorted in a snarky whisper.

Maybe Giles wasn't the best choice for this shoot. He clearly had his eye on Beckett for something more than just taking pictures, and he seemed like he was the type who got what he wanted.

"The only people he needs to impress are the casting directors," I said with as little emotion as possible. I didn't want Giles to know that he was really starting to piss me off. Thankfully, Beckett returned, now in jeans and a plain black sweater. Giles got him into position, and Beckett did a great job. I stood out of his line of sight, and Giles seemed much happier this time.

After we were done and Beckett had gone to change, I got the details from Giles about when the pictures would be ready and thanked him for all his help. I also made a note to find someone else for my future photography work.

"God, I felt like a piece of meat," Beckett said, shivering, as soon as we stepped out onto the street. "All he did was look at me like he was a lion and I was his lunch. It was creepy."

"Well, you did great, and we should have some stellar pictures out of this. I'm going to start lining up auditions, and I'll probably send you all over town. We need to get you in front of producers and casting directors. As I'm finding out, New York is a huge city, but the theater community is rather small. You have a solid résumé and a look that most don't have, so I suspect you'll turn heads."

Beckett shifted his gaze upward, and I followed it. "I thought I was being devoured."

"Get used to it," I said. "Once we get you out there, people will be watching you all the time." I smiled and motioned Beckett toward the avenue, where it would be easier to get a taxi. "God, I could use coffee," I groaned. I motioned toward the shop across the street. "Join me?"

"Sure," Beckett said. We crossed and walked into the busy shop. It seemed to be the end of the lunch rush, and by the time we got to the counter, most of the people had gotten what they came for and left. There were just a few tables with people lingering to talk. When we got our coffee, I glanced at the door and realized I wasn't interested in going back to the office. Not yet, anyway.

We sat down, and I sipped my latte. Beckett sat across from me and stared. I figured at any second he was going to remember who I was, but he just kept looking. "Sometimes I get this idea that I should know you from somewhere other than New York… like…."

"Mount Pleasant," I said, and then I sipped from my cup, watching him over the top.

"Yeah."

"So you really don't remember?" I figured I'd play with him to see how long it took.

"We do know each other?"

"Yes." I wasn't giving him anything more. "I looked very different in high school."

Beckett gasped and jumped to his feet. "You!" he exclaimed and pointed. "You knew all along." His eyes blazed hotter than they ever had during his audition or the photo session. "After what you did to me, I should—"

I chuckled uncomfortably. "What the hell are you talking about?" I remembered suddenly that we were in public and lowered my voice to a hiss. "You were the one who made my life miserable for months. Things were bad enough before you got involved, but after that it was open season."

"You weren't the one outed in front of everyone." Beckett headed for the door. I watched him go, then picked up my coffee and the bag with his clothes and raced out after him.

"What do you mean?" I demanded as I reached the sidewalk, thrusting the bag of clothes toward him. "I never did anything to you."

"You saw me... us... and told everyone."

"I most certainly did not." My anger rose and I stepped closer to Beckett, jamming my finger into his chest. "Yes, I saw you, but I left, and I never told a soul. I knew I was gay and wasn't about to out anyone. I have more class than that. I mean, even after the way you treated me, I was mature enough to realize that you had talent and signed you, against my better judgment. I should have let you rot on the garbage heap of obscurity." I turned away and began walking down the sidewalk. I'd had enough of this. Me outing him? He had no right to be angry with me. He wasn't the one who'd had all his self-confidence and worth stripped away layer by layer until there was nothing left at all.

A car horn honked and I was yanked backward, hard, falling against what I thought at first was a brick wall, the coffee sailing out of my hand.

"That car almost hit you."

I turned and found myself standing right in front of Beckett. I would have stepped back, but I'd have ended up in the street. I looked down, and of course, what was left of my coffee now lay on the sidewalk.

"I need to get back to my office." I needed distance. My heart pounded and I was still angry and liable to say something I would regret. "I'll be in contact as soon as I have some auditions for you." I turned and held my bag to my chest as I signaled for a cab. Getting out of here and away from Beckett as quickly as possible was my only goal.

A taxi pulled to the curb and I practically jumped in, giving him the office address as soon as I yanked the door closed. As the car took off, I sat back and tried to think about something other than Beckett.

The cab pulled up in front of the agency building, and I hurried inside and rode the elevator up. As soon as the doors parted, I marched out and past the reception desk. Millie looked up. She opened her mouth, then snapped it closed again and went back to her work. I continued to my office, closed the door, and flopped into the chair behind my desk. *How dare* he *be upset?* I wanted to bang my hands on the desk. Instead, I took a deep breath and picked up my phone, listened to the messages, and settled in to do my job. That was what I was here for, and regardless of Beckett's delusions or anything else, I would do my best for all my clients.

My phone rang as soon as I'd taken down my messages. "Yes."

"He's on his way back. I tried to stop him," Millie said, clearly frazzled. My door opened and Beckett lumbered in, face flushed, eyes blazing as though they'd been stoked with gasoline.

"It's okay," I told her and hung up. Then I turned my fury on Beckett. "What do you want?"

He tossed the bag of clothing on my chair and kicked the door closed. "I want to hear this crap once again about how you never said anything. How dare you just run away? Are you a coward? A scared rabbit?"

"No." I stood up. "I'm your agent, and I suggest you settle down and listen to yourself. I had nothing to do with outing you in high school. My guess is it was the guy who had your dick down his throat. Just because he couldn't talk while he was blowing you doesn't mean he didn't run his mouth afterward. Now I suggest you leave."

"You honestly didn't?" The heat and anger seemed to leech out of him by the second.

"Of course not," I said evenly. "You should go." Beckett nodded and turned, opening the door. "Don't forget your things," I told him, and he reached back and grabbed the bag before walking out.

I watched him for a few seconds and tried to get my head around what he'd said. Beckett actually thought I had been the one who outed him. I shook my head. I'd never do that to anyone. Maybe it was easier to blame me than someone he didn't want to think could hurt him. God, that little fact explained so very much. No wonder Beckett had been so mean—he'd hated me... for no reason to be sure, but he'd hated me for what he thought I'd done to him.

"You should have asked," I said quietly.

"Asked what?" Garren said as he came into my office.

"Nothing," I answered quickly. "What can I do for you?"

"We heard loud voices and thought you might need help," Garren said as he looked around.

"I'm fine. It was just a difference of opinion. Nothing to be worried about." I sat back down. "How are things going for you?"

Garren shrugged. "The usual." He kept looking at me. I wondered what he wanted. "I was wondering if you'd like to get dinner or something sometime. We haven't had a chance to talk or anything much since you got here other than to glare or yell at each other." Garren smiled. I figured this was his way of trying to build bridges after our disagreement over the client. "I'll call you and set something up."

"That'd be great," I said. I watched Garren leave, then sat back down and got to work. I had plenty to do, and thankfully I didn't spend more than a few seconds wondering about Beckett Huntington.

"So how did it go at work?" Val asked as he sat on my sofa late that evening. He'd knocked on my door when he got home and since I was still up, I invited him in.

"Okay," I answered pensively.

Val picked up the yearbook I'd pulled out of one of the boxes under my bed. "Taking a walk down memory lane?"

"More like Elm Street. High school was a nightmare."

Val set the yearbook down. "That wouldn't have anything to do with a certain client of yours, would it?"

"Possibly." I sat down next to Val and handed him a beer. "Sorry, I don't have the stuff for cocktails. I hope this is okay."

Val opened it and took a drink. "Perfect." He smiled and waited expectantly. I tried to ignore him, but he stared at me without saying anything. It was unnerving, to say the least. "You might as well spill, because I'm just going to sit here until you do."

"Why is this so important to you?"

"Who doesn't love gossip?" Val took another chug of his beer. "Besides, I know there's more to this than you're saying. I think you're attracted to this guy and don't want to admit it. He gets under your skin because you have the hots for him. That's the only reason you're so obsessed with him."

"I am not."

"You keep telling yourself that. But every time we've gotten together since you saw him at the gym, he's the topic of conversation, and that's never happened before with any guy."

"He's just so…." I tried to find the words while Val smiled at me indulgently.

"Protest all you want. I know what I know."

I wanted to wring his neck, but I couldn't very well do that when he was fucking right. "Can we just drop it?"

"As long as you admit he's hot and that you like him."

I signed. "Okay, he's really hot. But I do not like him. He's a complete ass. He actually accused me of outing him in school. The pain in the ass. He thought I outed him and that's why he made my life miserable."

Val rubbed his hands together. "Honey, you have him where you want him."

"How so?"

"Guilt. Let me tell you, it's a wonderful thing. You're his agent—"

"I would never let this interfere with doing my job," I growled, cutting him off. "I'm a professional, and regardless of how I feel about the gorilla personally, I will do my best for him professionally. All you have in this business is your reputation. It's what we trade on, and I will not have that endangered for any reason."

Val set down his bottle. "Take off the coat of righteous indignation and listen to me. I only meant that he can't avoid you. So make the most of what he did."

"I wish he'd never crossed my path." I was beginning to think Beckett was my own personal black cat. Every time we met, I ended up getting sent flying and landing on my proverbial ass.

"But he did."

"Let's talk about something else. Are you and Rod still going out this weekend?"

"Yeah. He wants to get together earlier, but with the shifts I'm working, I don't think it's possible. I hate this shift. I get stuff done in the morning, but by the time I get home in the evening it's really too late to get together with anyone if they have to get up at a normal time."

"How long do you have to work this shift?" I asked.

The front door buzzer sounded, and I looked up. I stilled. Val did the same. I wasn't expecting anyone, so I got up with Val behind me and cracked open my door, peering toward the iron-fronted glass door of the building. There were also windows on either side, so it was easy to see anyone standing outside.

"It looks like you have a visitor," Val said cheekily. "Do you want me to stay?"

"No." I wondered what in the heck Beckett was doing out in front of my building.

"Okay." Val walked by me to the front door, then opened it to allow Beckett inside. "You call me if you need anything." He glared at Beckett, and I had to stop myself from laughing as the notion of a mouse glaring at a cat came to mind. Val turned as though he were covered in armor and walked up the stairs.

"What are you doing here?" I asked Beckett once I heard Val's door close. Crossing my arms across my chest, I waited for him to answer me.

"The Internet is amazing," he answered.

"Okay. That explains how you found me, but what are you doing here?" I wouldn't let him off the hook.

"I went home and then wandered the neighborhood, thinking about things and some of the stuff I did back in high school." Beckett closed the front door to the building, and I stepped back into my apartment. I didn't invite Beckett in—I was wondering if I wanted him here at all. But since I didn't tell him to leave, Beckett slowly came inside. I didn't sit, so he stood just inside the door. "I have to ask—you really didn't say anything about what you saw?"

I shook my head. "What does it matter? You had a few tough weeks and then you were as popular as you'd been before. Sure, some kids avoided you, but the team backed you, and the girls loved you even more."

"That was at school. That little revelation meant I had to change homes... again." Beckett looked like someone had kicked his puppy. "I was seventeen at the time—not an adult. Three months from my eighteenth birthday."

"Your parents kicked you out?"

"No. My parents were dead. They had been for six years. I lived with my grandmother until she died, and then I spent much of high school in a foster home. I thought they loved me, but as soon as they heard what was going around school, they called child services and said I was incompatible with their family. So I ended up moving again, this time into a county home. No parents, just an overseer, as I referred to her. I shared a room with another boy. I moved out as soon as I turned eighteen and went on welfare. I had nothing and got into the college by the grace of God."

I had no idea what to say. I motioned to my chair. It was sturdy enough to support him. Then I sat on the sofa. I really needed to get something to cover its ugliness. "I didn't know."

"Well, I didn't give anyone the chance to know. I covered it with personality to most people and blamed you for everything that happened." Beckett cleared his throat. "Then I heard that you were trying out for the lead in the school play and that you were the only one up for the part. So I figured, how hard could it be? And I tried out. I was thrilled that I'd been able to take the part away from you. I knew you wanted it bad. It was written on your face, and when I got the part, I was happy as hell. I'd taken it away from you with no effort at all."

"Yeah, I know," I said, remembering the ache and hurt. What I'd wanted had been so close, but my tormentor had taken it all away with what looked like ease. "That day ended my acting career. I loved it. But I wasn't good enough. I realized that. I had planned to major in theater in college but ended up changing to business and worked backstage. And you got your revenge on someone who never did you any harm."

"Yeah," Beckett breathed. "I realize I was wrong."

"You think?"

"Well, I'm not angry at the world the way I used to be. I know it's no consolation, but I figured out years ago that my anger led me to my calling. I found a talent, but I didn't major in theater either. I took classes and loved it, though. But I don't remember you after high school."

"I decided I didn't want to be Pay-*ton* anymore. I lost weight—"

"I noticed. I didn't recognize you."

"Yeah. Once the weight came off and my skin firmed up, I didn't look the same at all. The chins were gone and the shape of my face seemed to change. I wasn't as round anywhere. I remember seeing you around, but I stayed out of your way. I wanted to be someone different, and you were a reminder of the person I used to be."

"So you saw me?"

"Sometimes. I worked quite a few productions because I loved it, but then I stepped away from it. After I graduated, I got a job as an assistant theater manager in Ann Arbor. I stayed for a while, then tried for jobs here in the city. I still love the theater, but I knew I wasn't good enough to be an actor. By a stroke of luck, I got this job, and I think I'm really good at it."

Beckett nodded. "Then why did you take me as a client?"

"I wasn't going to until I saw your audition. If you hadn't been so fucking good, I would have said thank you and showed you the door. But you are good, and I'd be a fool if I let my personal feelings get in the way of business. So I set them aside and did what was best for both of us."

"You're a better person than I am... than I was," Beckett said softly. "During college and after I started competing, I used my theater to make my poses and routines dramatic, and I started to win. I got bigger and bigger and won more and more."

"Why'd you stop?"

"It wasn't what I wanted from my life. When you're young, you can win. As you get older, it requires chemical help, and I wasn't going to go there. I got some roles in community theater and then decided I had nothing to lose, so I moved here, staying with a friend. I got a few small roles, and Jane saw me and thought I might have promise."

"Well, you do." I got up and went to the refrigerator. I needed another beer. I brought one for Beckett as well, because it would have been rude not to. He took it and rolled the bottle between his hands.

"Was I really that mean to you?" Beckett asked.

I opened the bottle. "Yes, you were. I was a kid, another person, and you delighted in making sure I was the butt of everyone else's jokes. I gained weight because of medication, and it was hard not to eat when comfort was all I wanted." I drank half the bottle in a few gulps. "Every day was hell, and though my parents were supportive, they didn't know everything that was happening." I stood and walked to where Beckett sat. "You made me feel so badly about myself that I actually thought about ending it all more than once."

Beckett gasped.

"You have no idea how many times I wished I could have you right where you are now, right in front of me, so I could tell you what I thought of you."

Beckett swallowed, put his beer bottle down, and crossed his arms over his chest. "Then why don't you?"

I realized there was no reason to. Not anymore. "Because all the anger and hurt is in the past. Yes, it was painful, but I can't carry it with me forever. It isn't healthy, and when I shed the weight, I'd like to think I shed the person I was along with it."

Beckett stared at me, openmouthed. "You have to be shitting me. No one is that nice."

"I never said I was nice. I just had to let it go or it would eat me alive." I took a deep breath. "That's what my dad told me to do. Of course it wasn't that easy." And now I was acting my ass off because I didn't want him to think I was a basket case or something. Beckett had an immense impact on my life, mostly negatively, but I was who I was because of all the experiences in my life. I couldn't change that, and I wasn't going to hold on to the past.

"That's more than I could ever do," Beckett admitted. "I spent my entire life afraid someone would look at me and see me for who I really was, and you... you're so damned comfortable just being you."

"I am not," I said, more loudly than I intended. "There are things I hate about myself."

"Like what?" Beckett asked, sitting back. The fucker looked relaxed. He seemed to be enjoying himself. He even reached for the beer and opened it.

"It's easy for me to say that I've moved on and that I can turn my back on what happened. I'd really like to think I'm that kind of person. I want to be, but in truth I'm finding it hard. I know carrying a whole bunch of baggage will only weigh me down, and I want to let it go. But saying it and doing it are very different things."

"You don't have to be some kind of saint. Hell, I certainly know I'm not."

"That's easy for you to say. I know differently." I emptied my beer and got up for another, opening it before flopping back down in the chair.

"How many of those have you had?" Beckett asked.

I shrugged. My memory was becoming a little hazy. I knew I'd had a few sitting in front of the television and one with Val, then these. Maybe that accounted for the way I was running off at the mouth, but at that point, I didn't much care. I popped off the top.

"Maybe you should take it easy."

"Maybe you should stop acting so nice—you make it hard for me to hate you." I drank some from the bottle, then stood and walked over to where Beckett sat. He still held his bottle. I leaned over him. "I should really hate you. You know that." God, I was on a roll, and the small part of me not influenced by the alcohol said to stop, but the rest of me was sliding downhill, picking up steam. "You were such a shit to me in school, and I just want to hit you." So I did. I smacked Beckett on the shoulder. "Ow," I said, waving my hand. "You got rocks in there?"

"Yeah," Beckett chuckled. "I got rocks in my shirt. Maybe I should go."

"No. You need to hear this. You were a total shit to me, and I hate you. I hate the way you treated me, and I hate that you took away my chance at acting. I never did anything to you except watch you like a lovesick kid, and you shit all over me." I waved the bottle around and then took another drink. "I hate that you're so fucking talented and all I can do is watch, and I hate the way I feel about you." I stepped back and put my hand over my mouth. "Maybe you should go." Rationality had to make an appearance, and as soon as the words crossed my lips it was like someone had doused me with cold water. "Oh fuck." I turned away, unable to look at him.

"What did you mean?" Beckett asked.

"It doesn't matter." I hated that I'd let my guard down. "Just forget it."

"What if I don't want to? You're a nice guy."

"And we get shit on all the time." I should have known not to drink so much. When I did, I always hit this point where my mouth engaged and suddenly I'd say anything. I always remembered what I said, but I couldn't control it at the time. Then, as more alcohol hit me, I started to get weepy and maudlin as hell. That was the worst part.

"Are you a 'feel sorry for yourself' drunk?" Beckett asked.

"No," I said loudly. "I'm just a depressing drunk." And so much more.

"What did you mean?" He stood, and I heard him come up behind me. I didn't turn around, even though I wanted to so badly. "You can tell me. I promise I'll keep it to myself."

I laughed. "No one ever keeps anything embarrassing about someone else to themselves. They tell everyone."

"You didn't. Remember? You said you saw me with Peter and didn't tell anyone."

I lifted the beer and drank a few swallows. What the hell, it was already open, and it was going to be my last one. "I never told anyone. Not even my friends. They asked what I'd done to get you mad at me, and I never said a thing. I could have, but I didn't." My voice slurred slightly, the beer going to my head.

"So what did you mean?"

I turned around. Beckett was so close I could feel his heat. I closed my eyes and swayed a little on my feet. I'd definitely had enough, so I handed Beckett the bottle. He set it aside and turned back to me. "Come on," I said. "Look at you. Geez." I reached out and my hand came into contact with his chest of stone. When he didn't pull away, I slid my fingers around one of the buttons of his button-down shirt. Fabric gave way to smooth skin and I wiggled my fingers, excitement coursing through me. "You're like this god-man. Sexy and all that." I loved the tantalizing touch of how he felt, and I wanted more. I was hard, and one of my legs began to shake like a dog's when you pet it just right.

This was bad and I knew it, but I didn't care. At least not at that moment. "You're really sexy, okay?" I whispered. "You're hot. And sexy, did I mention that?" I knew I was in trouble when I started to giggle. But as soon as I looked up and saw the heat in his eyes, I forgot everything else. "I used to be really fat and I hated myself, so I lost weight. Wanna see?" I stepped back and tugged my shirt over my head. "See? I'm not fat anymore."

"You should sit down before you fall down."

"If I do, will you catch me?" I giggled again. "I hate it when I'm like this. I swear I will tell anyone anything they want to know." I made it to the sofa and sat down.

"What did you mean that you used to watch me?" Beckett loomed over me, but he was smiling.

"Pffft. Like you don't know you're sex on a stick. Everyone watched you. It doesn't mean anything."

"But you said you watched me in high school."

"Of course I did. I was gay, and you were hot… are hot…. God, you're getting me all confused. Did I say you should go? That might be a good idea now."

"Maybe. And maybe leaving isn't such a good idea until you tell me what you meant." There was an edge to Beckett's voice.

"Okay. I think you're hot, and sometimes I stay awake at night, thinking about you. I used to do that in high school too. Once I had to go into the locker room when you were changing for practice. I whacked off thinking about you for weeks after that." Maybe if I told him all of it, it would gross him out and he'd leave. "I thought about you the past few nights too."

Cool air flowed over my skin. I looked around for my shirt. I was going from hot to cold every few minutes, and by the time I remembered where my shirt was I was warm again.

"You did?"

"Yeah."

When Beckett leaned closer, I licked my lips and looked away.

He lightly touched my chin and turned my head until I was looking at him again. "Did you think that would make me mad?"

I shrugged. I didn't know what to think with him touching me and the scent of him filling my nose. He smelled like a drug I was addicted to and couldn't possibly get enough of. Those kinds of things are bad for you, and I knew I should push him away.

"I'm not the same man I was then, and neither are you," he said.

"I know I'm not as fat."

"Yes, there's that. But you're confident, and that's sexy too," Beckett said.

I blinked up at him. God, his blue eyes were so pretty, and the way he looked at me sent shivers of hot and cold shooting up my spine at the same time. A whimper formed in my throat, but I swallowed it down. I had to.

"I am not," I whispered without conviction, hoping secretly that Beckett did find me attractive, because then I might know what it would feel like to actually touch him. Beckett reached out to me, clasping my shoulders in his large hands. I closed my eyes and my attention centered on the two spots where he touched me. His thumbs made little circles at the top of my chest, and I wanted to whimper, wishing he'd take me into his arms. Beckett could probably snap me like a twig whenever he chose, but I wasn't scared.

"What do you want?" he asked. I slid my eyes open. "What do you think about when you're alone at night, dreaming of me?"

"Don't be mean to me. Just go," I whispered. "I just want to be alone."

Beckett tugged me forward. When his lips touched mine, I thought I was being burned. My head clouded with lust and desire, blotting out the haze of alcohol. I wrapped my arms around Beckett's neck, pulling him in hard as I kissed him back. I was demanding, filling the kiss with need and the desire I'd always felt but had been afraid would never be returned. When he backed away, I thought he was leaving. I grabbed his shirt and yanked him back, tugging at it until the buttons gave way, and the fabric parted under my hands. I let go and slipped my hands under his shirt. Hard muscles flexed and danced under my touch. The planes of Beckett's chest quivered, and when I found his nipples, I bumped my fingers over the hardening nubs.

He kissed me harder, tightening his grip on my shoulders. I let him bring me closer, my chest pressing to his as he took possession of my mouth. It was exactly what I wanted. My head swam, and when we parted, I gasped for breath.

It was hard to breathe or see straight. I slid my hands under his shirt again, around to his back. He felt amazingly strong, and I held him to me, resting my head on his shoulder. "Is this real?"

"Yes." He slid an arm under my knees and lifted me as though I weighed nothing, then carried me across the room to the bed. He laid me on it and I tugged him down, kissing him again, pulling at his shirt. I wanted to feel him against me, but when I clutched at him, he held me back. I sighed and groaned softly as he pushed away, stroking my chest. I had to close my eyes to take in the sensation. I willed him to give me everything I wanted and to take me places I'd only dreamed of.

He kissed me and I relaxed. Warmth surrounded me, and I curled into it, holding on to it. I wanted it to last forever. "Good night," Beckett whispered.

"Good night, sexy man. Just hold me." I felt his hand on my arm and sighed. I was warm and safe. Then my consciousness slipped away and everything went black and still.

I didn't know how much later I jerked upright in bed. My head ached and my mouth was dry as a bone. I was alone, and all the doors were closed and locked. Blankets had been drawn up around me, and my shirt lay folded on the seat of the chair. Everything was as it should be except that I felt more lonely and cold than I could remember being in a very long time. I got up, used the bathroom, and drank some water before returning to bed.

CHAPTER 4—LINGERING

THE NEXT two days passed in a daze. I'd gotten a taste and a touch of Beckett, and whenever I wasn't occupied with something else, my mind returned to each moment, no matter how hazy. I received proofs of Beckett's photographs, and they were amazing. Now that they were ready, I got on the phone and made some calls.

"Payton," Gloria said as she knocked on my doorframe. "I have a lead for you. That young man you just signed... I think I have a deal that could include him. They need someone to play a love interest. They specified a man who is breathtakingly handsome. It goes without saying that he has to be able to act." Gloria handed me a card. "A lot of people will be interested in the role because this could be a blockbuster. I told Julia that you'd call. That's her number. Arrange it right away and cut everyone else off. They're going to put the call out on Monday."

I grinned, already dialing the number as I thanked her. "Julia, it's Payton Gowan."

Julia chuckled. "Gloria said you'd be calling. But I wasn't expecting the call that fast. We thought we had the part cast but the actor dropped out because he got a better offer. I need to cast this part right away, so how quickly can you get your client in to see us?"

"When do you need him?" I asked. I'd pedal Beckett down on a bicycle if I had to.

"Can you get him here in two hours?" She gave me the address of the theater.

"I'll call you back. Give me fifteen minutes at the outside." I disconnected, heart pounding as I looked up Beckett's number. I dialed it and the phone went to voice mail. "It's Pay. I have a possible audition for a play. Things are happening fast, and I need you to call me back right away." I recited the number and hung up, glancing at the clock. I willed my phone to ring, but it stayed silent. In five minutes I called again and got voice mail one more time. "Call me now."

I was about to call Julia back and put my career on the line to promise that Beckett would be there when my phone rang. I snatched it up.

"Payton? This is Beckett."

"Damn, man, you're killing me here. Always keep your phone on and charged. I have an audition for you. It's in less than two hours. Get down to my office right away and I'll give you all the details. They're in a bit of a panic, and I got an inside track. They want a real looker, so make sure you come dressed to kill." I checked the clock. "I'll call you right back." I hung up and called Julia back. "We'll be there at eleven," I told her. "Can you messenger a script over?"

"Gloria has a copy."

"Okay. We'll be prepared to knock your socks off."

"I hope so," she said skeptically. "I'll see you then." She hung up, and I hurried down to Gloria's office. She was in conference, so I settled for her assistant, Marvin.

"Marvin, do you happen to have a copy of *Make My Day*?"

He opened a file drawer and pulled out the script. "I need this one, but I'll make you a copy and run it down." He was already pulling it apart as he got up from his desk. "Give me ten minutes." He hurried away and I went back to my office. I had the script for Beckett, and I had the time we were supposed to be there. Now I just needed him to get here. There wasn't much time for him to get familiar with the play.

My phone rang again. One of my clients, Janice, hadn't gotten the part she wanted, but they were offering an alternate, so I made the call and encouraged her to accept. "They have agreed to let you understudy for the countess."

"All right. I need this job," Janice said.

"You know how things work. You have what they need, so if the show is a hit, you'll move up."

"Fingers crossed," she said.

"I know," I told her. "You're amazing, and we're building your reputation."

"Thanks… for everything. Jane hadn't gotten me a part in three months, and you did it in a week. You're awesome!" Once she hung up, I smiled. Things were working out. At least for now. I had to add that to myself. Usually right about the time things started going well, they all fell apart.

I picked up the phone and asked Millie to send Beckett back when he came in. A few minutes later he was in my doorway.

"Come in, sit down. I have the script and you need to get familiar with it. You're playing Chad. He's a Lothario and romances away Frederick's daughter, Caroline. She's the only person who matters in his life, and you take her away."

"Is that all there is to the part?"

"No. It seems you really do fall in love with her, and at the end, both of you return when Frederick needs you both. To him you're taking away his daughter, and the play is written from his perspective, but once that changes at the end, it's just her living her life and everything has been told through his distorted lens."

"Sounds pretty powerful," Beckett said as he settled back and opened the script.

"Play it that way. This isn't a comedy, but a serious drama. But if there is a line where you can interject some light humor… well, you never know." I checked the clock. "You prepare, and I'm going to make arrangements for a car to take us there."

Beckett closed the script. "You're going to go?"

"I don't have to, but I thought a friendly face would be good." I smiled quickly. "Now go back to work. You need to blow her socks off."

"The producer is a woman?"

"The casting director is, and she's the one you need to impress, at least this time." I motioned for him to get back to it as I reviewed and cleared my e-mail and told Millie I was going to be out of the office for a while. I made sure to send a thank-you note to Gloria.

When Millie called to say the car was waiting, I led Beckett out and down to street level. The last thing I wanted was for him to be late.

Traffic was a nightmare, and we weren't getting anywhere quickly.

"What do we do?" Beckett asked over the assault of car horns and yelling.

"We'll walk if we have to," I told him. I was about to get out when the cars in front of us began to move.

"The bus ahead finally moved out of the way," the driver said. We got through the intersection and the next one as well. We pulled up in front of the theater and rushed inside.

Places like this had always been magical for me, but right now everything was dark. On show nights, the lobby would be bright, and the rich colors of the decades-old space would glow with warmth and reflect the excitement and anticipation of every theatergoer. But right now, with the lights off and the space empty, the theater seemed like a lady all dressed up and waiting for a date that she wasn't sure was going to show.

A woman entered from the theater proper.

"I'm Pay Gowan," I said, "and this is Beckett Huntington."

"Right on time. I like that. Julia Richards. Let's get started." She turned and walked us down the dimly lit aisle, past the red seats for the audience and under a lavishly appointed balcony to the stage. I sat down and watched as she motioned Beckett to the stage, where a young woman already stood waiting. "Grace will read opposite you, so just hand her your script," Julia said as she took a seat a few rows behind me.

Grace looked a little taken aback when she realized Beckett held the script from the play being produced. I wasn't sure what scene he'd chosen, but Grace began to read, and Beckett went into a scene that he'd first read less than two hours earlier. It was a powerful section of the play where Chad woos Caroline.

My heart stopped more than once in the two or three minutes he was on stage. Readers for auditions usually simply read, but Beckett pulled her into the scene, speaking the lines to her as though she were

Caroline, moving closer at just the right moments. I shifted to the edge of my seat, leaning closer as I tried to figure out if Chad was actually going to kiss her or not. For those few minutes, Beckett was transported and changed into Chad, and I wished more than anything that I was Grace so he would tell *me* those beautiful words about how the world would be dull and colorless without me. I saw Chad's passion and conviction reflected in Beckett, and then he leaned in to kiss her, but stopped just short. I held my breath and stilled as neither of them moved.

The spell broke with a sound from out front, and I heard someone say, "Thank you." I got up and walked toward the sound. Julia stood and came down the aisle toward me.

"I was expecting that I'd be here alone, but the director and producer are both here." She motioned to seats near the two men, and I took one.

"Thank you, Mr. Huntington, that was impressive," the director called out to Beckett.

"I could have done better, but I only got the script a couple of hours ago," Beckett said. I smiled. He looked amazing on that stage, filling it with his presence. I wanted to go up there with him to bask in the glow that seemed to surround him.

"You're bigger, physically, than we anticipated using."

I had expected this reaction and handed Julia the portfolio of photographs. She opened it and smiled, then stood and walked down the aisle to the director. I saw her point out one picture in the group, and the director and producer shared a look. I knew Beckett had the part in that moment. I just did. They had seen exactly the answer they were looking for.

"Can you dance, Mr. Huntington?" the director asked.

I couldn't for the life of me remember if we'd covered that or not. We were so close, and I was seconds from biting my nails to the quick. *God, no wonder agents don't normally attend auditions.* If I did this all the time, I'd be a complete nervous wreck on a daily basis.

"Do you have music?" Beckett asked.

"Can we have the music we were going to use for act two?" the director called to someone in the back, and the music began. Beckett walked over to Grace, put an arm around her waist, and glided her around the stage with grace and fluidity. Jesus Christ, I was starting to feel jealous of Grace. She flushed slightly in Beckett's arms as they moved.

"Thank you," the director called, and the music stopped. "Can you sing?" he asked.

"Passably. It's not my greatest strength."

They'd never said this was a musical. I nearly panicked. We were so close.

"That's all right. This isn't a musical. I just had to make sure you weren't perfect." There was humor in his voice. "Young man, please don't change your hair or look at all. No beards or some such thing. Are you open to a change of hairstyle if required?"

"Of course," Beckett answered from the edge of the stage with so much excitement in his voice he looked about ready to jump down at them any second. He leaned forward in anticipation, and I did the same, willing them to say he had the part.

"Thank you for coming in. We really appreciate it."

I sat back in my seat, stunned. I had been so sure he had everything they wanted. I turned to Julia, who was already moving back toward them. She and the two men conferred, and she lifted the portfolio and brought it back to me. "They would like to speak with you."

I nodded and went over to the producer and director while Beckett descended from the stage. "Payton Gowan," I said as I approached.

"Hiram McTavish. I'm the director, and this is William Howard, our producer." I shook hands with both men. I had, of course, heard of both of them and was thrilled to meet them. I had heard there was a story behind Hiram's name. Apparently his mother was Jewish and his father Scottish. Only in New York.

"He's not what we were expecting for the role, physically," Mr. Howard said. "But we like him otherwise and his preparation was amazing. Did he really only see the script a couple of hours ago?"

"Yes. I gave it to him."

Mr. Howard extended his hand again. "Your client has the part. We'll be in touch as far as the contracts and details soon." I nodded and handed each of them one of my cards. "We appreciate you being available on such short notice." He turned to where Beckett was standing. "If he can produce a performance like that in a few hours, I'm anxious to see what he'll do in rehearsal. We'll be in touch."

"Thank you," I said, grinning. Julia led me to where Beckett was waiting, and we left the theater.

"You got the part," I told him as soon as we were out on the street. "They're going to send me the details, and we'll go over them thoroughly. I suspect it's a limited engagement. I believe the show is expected to run for just six or eight weeks."

"So I only have a job for two months?" he asked.

"This is theater. The show could close after one night. You never know. But the script is good, and I think you'll have a good run." I looked up at the marquee and smiled. "You're going to have a stellar run." We had been in such a hurry that I hadn't been able to do my usual research. "Look who we're going to be working with—Kendall Monroe. I'd heard he was interested in doing theater again."

"Are you kidding? I love him." Beckett grinned.

"This is a great part, and you'll make the most of it. Then we'll turn it into something else. Just do your best. You had what they wanted and blew them away. And don't think they aren't going to tell everyone they know about how you played a scene from their play at an audition with only two hours' prep. They're still wondering how you did that." Hell, so was I.

"I have a good imagination," Beckett said, his gaze burning into me so deeply I thought my knees would give out. I tugged at my collar. The wind was calm, thank goodness, but it was still chilly outside. However, I was getting warmer by the second. "You remember what happened the other night?"

I stood stock-still. "Most of it, I think." I lied. I remembered every second my hands were in contact with his skin and each time he kissed me. They were indelibly etched on my brain. How could I touch him and not remember it?

"I remember all of it," he said in a bedroom voice that sent a quiver through me. All I could think of was that I had to get away, and yet I wanted to move closer. "You ripping my shirt because you wanted to get to me. The way your hand felt on my chest." Beckett moved closer. If I didn't find a way to get out from under his gaze, I was going to pass out from lack of oxygen.

The car pulled up. I had forgotten to call him, but the driver must have been intuitive because he had amazing timing. I pulled the door open and got inside. Beckett followed, and the driver pulled out into traffic.

I sat back in my seat, staring at my knees and then Beckett's knees. After that I was so screwed. There was nothing to stop me from lifting my gaze slightly to his thighs and the way his jeans tightened over them, like denim-encased tree trunks.

"Are you staring at my package?" Beckett whispered. I jerked my head around, looking out the window. The thing was, I had been. How could I not? It was right there, and it wasn't as though it could be missed. Beckett laughed and placed his hand on my thigh, squeezing lightly. "I was teasing and yet I wasn't."

"I got that." What I didn't understand was the way I couldn't take my eyes off him. I'd turned to look out the window, but my gaze was drawn back to him like a magnet. No wonder he'd gotten the part. The way his black shirt stretched across his chest was nearly obscene, and from this angle, the light fabric followed each angle of his body. I closed my eyes and felt my fingers moving over his nipples just like they had the other night.

"What are you thinking about right now?" Beckett asked, soft enough that only I could hear.

How could I answer that question? I was thinking about that night and how he'd brought me to bed. He was so strong, but he'd held me gently, as if I was precious.

"This is so wrong," I whispered. "I'm your agent and we have a professional relationship. At least we're supposed to." I was acting so stupid. "I need time to think." At least that was what I said. Of course what I wanted was to direct the driver back to my apartment and spend the rest of the day in bed with Beckett. Maybe if I could get this whole thing out of my system, I could think about something other than him for five minutes.

Beckett clasped my leg and then released it. We pulled up in front of my office, and Beckett got out with me.

"Don't you need to go home or to work?"

"It's my day off at the grocery store. I was wondering if there was a conference room or something I could use. It's hard for me to get anything done at home. I just have the sofa and there's always someone there."

"I'm not sure." I shrugged. "As you saw, my office is tiny, and the conference rooms are often in demand, but I'll see if I can work something out." Space in Manhattan was always at a premium, and I understood that the agency didn't pay for any more space than they absolutely needed. Apparently, before I joined the firm, my tiny office had acted as a conference space.

I escorted Beckett up to the twelfth floor and into the office.

"How did it go?" Millie asked.

"Very productive," I told her. "He got the part, and I know they're anxious to get down to business, so is there a space he can use to work for a few hours?" I knew this was an unusual request, but other agents had brought their clients in for one reason or another. Claude had explained to me when I first joined the firm that, depending on the day, an agent was a babysitter, coach, psychologist, agent, and parent.

"Jane's office has been cleaned out, and it's empty at the moment. We aren't using it for anything other than conferences for now, so you could put him in there."

I thanked her before walking Beckett down to the empty office next to mine.

"I have a lot of work to do, but I'll let you know as soon as I hear anything." I pulled myself away from him and went back to my office, closing the door and breathing a sigh of relief.

I was making calls when Garren stuck his head in. "Lunch?"

I had been putting him off for some reason, but now I nodded. I didn't really trust him. Maybe it was the residue of the incident a few weeks earlier. I wasn't sure, but my gut urged caution. I finished my call arranging for another audition, and then I called my client with the information before hanging up.

Garren was still hanging around, and once I finished my call, he came inside. "Is your client using Jane's office?"

"Yes," I answered. "He needed space to prep for a role."

Millie came in with a package and handed it to me. "It came by messenger." I opened it and grinned as I glanced through the contract. They evidently did want Beckett. Their terms were generous.

"Can you give me half an hour?" I asked Garren.

Garren nodded and left as I took the contract to Beckett and closed the door to Jane's office. When I gave him the news, I had to caution him not to yell. He jumped up anyway, and I was engulfed in immensely strong arms, lifted off my feet, and twirled around the tiny space. "You need to put me down so we can go over the offer."

"All right," Beckett said and moved away.

"Come to my office and we'll go over the details." I still held the contract, but I wasn't about to go over it in here. This space was dead—or at least it felt dead. I opened the door, and Beckett followed me next door, to my office. He sat in my extra chair, but immediately bounced back to his feet. "If you don't settle down everyone in the building is going to think we're having an earthquake." I laughed. I was happy for him. Hell, I was happy, period.

"You look confused," Beckett told me.

"Sorry." I kind of was.

"Why?"

"Because I'm happy for you, and…."

"You feel like you shouldn't be because of what I did," Beckett supplied.

"Yeah, sort of, I guess. I've been a little out of sorts lately, and it has nothing to do with you. It's my problem, and I'm the one who needs to work through it. Today, this"—I pointed to the contract—"is about you. The part is yours, and they went above the equity minimum for a part like this, which is great. It says they thought you were dynamite. The run is expected to be six weeks, and you open in three. There is a possible extension for two additional weeks at the end of the run. It's Broadway, and landing a role like this could make your career."

"So you think I should sign?"

"Yes, and once you do, I'm going to do my best to get everyone I can think of into that theater to see you. This is the opportunity you've been waiting for, so make the most of it." I handed him a pen and the contract, and he signed at the bottom. I added my signature where required, as well as the agency information.

"Now what do I do?" he asked when we were done.

"I have a lunch appointment with one of the other agents. Come along with us to celebrate and then go on home and tell all your friends and family about your upcoming Broadway debut."

"Do things usually work this way?"

I laughed. "God, no. I think the last time it happened was with Shirley Jones and Richard Rodgers. So take the gifts the universe hands you and be grateful." As soon as those words were out of my mouth, it hit me. I was quick to give advice but I rarely took my own. Maybe Beckett was one of the gifts I should be taking. Then again, maybe he was the apple of temptation.

I packaged up the contract and excused myself, taking it to Millie so she could record it for me and arrange to messenger it back.

"I see you're the one who's been keeping my assistant so busy," Claude said from his office.

"Stop it," Millie told him. "He's doing well and you know it." She took the package and promised she'd take care of it for me. "Don't listen to him." She turned toward Claude's office. "If I only had to work with Claude all day, I'd probably go postal on him." She winked at me. "If he picks on you, he likes you," she added in a whisper.

A snort came from Claude's office. I thanked her again. Garren was outside my office waiting, and I got Beckett before leaving the office. "He just signed his first contract, and we're celebrating," I told Garren. I wasn't sure how he felt about Beckett joining us, but it was only lunch, and a barrier between Garren and me was probably good.

We went just around the corner to a deli. I found out what Beckett wanted and placed our orders while he snagged us a table. Even after the regular lunch hour, the place was busy.

"I understand you've had a really good few weeks," Garren said to me when we sat down with our sandwiches. "I remember those first few successes. They seem like everything is going your way, and then…."

"I think Pay is doing a great job and takes care with his clients. He'll always do well," Beckett said. "People appreciate someone willing to go the extra mile. And that's Pay. It's what he does and it will carry him far." Beckett took a bite of his sandwich, and I glanced at him out of the corner of my eyes, smiling slightly.

"Aww, isn't that cute," Garren said snidely. I glared at him. Garren looked away first and ate as a cover. I was not going to allow him to treat anyone like that, least of all one of my clients. I made a note never to go to lunch with Garren again. Whatever crap he was peddling, I wasn't going to buy it.

"So is there anything interesting you're working on?" I asked him.

"There's a big musical about to open, and I've got a couple of clients up for really good parts." He sounded so smug. "*Carried Away.* I'm expecting to hear anytime."

"I heard this morning," I said. "One of my clients landed the role of Candice and is understudying for the countess."

Garren didn't say anything, but I saw his jaw tighten.

"I suspect they'll be making all their calls very soon." I had no idea what roles he was referring to, but I guessed Janice had snagged that one out from under his client. "I've got performances to attend all weekend. Prospective clients to see in action." It seemed some of my new clients were spreading the word.

"I haven't been to the theater as an audience member in years," Beckett said.

"I've gone so many times that the last time I almost didn't enjoy it. I go to watch the actors and judge performances rather than to enjoy myself," Garren said.

"You don't really like it?" I asked.

Garren shrugged. "It'll happen to you too. You'll get to the point where the whole thing becomes a business, and once that happens, it sucks the fun out of it."

I turned to Beckett, then back to Garren. I hoped like hell that never happened to me. "I still remember the first time I got to go to a real play. My dad took me. He said the play was too advanced for me, but he wanted to go, so he took me. I remember watching the spectacle from the first moment the curtain parted. Yeah, Chekhov was a little advanced, but I was enthralled. The theatrical magic has never faded for me, even after some heartbreaks. They were my own and I had to deal with them, but they weren't because of the theater." I shared a quick glance with Beckett.

"What was your disappointment?" Garren asked, and I instantly wished I hadn't gone there.

"The day I realized I wasn't as good an actor as I thought I was. I switched my gifts to backstage and the business side. I thought about giving up the theater altogether, but my dad said I shouldn't. So I wasn't going to be a great actor—I could be the best director, producer, or agent there was. I helped run a small theater and then got this job. What about you?"

"I sort of fell into it," Garren answered sullenly. "My mom and dad were show people in Vegas, so it was expected that I'd go into the business as well. I didn't want to be on the stage, so I got into this."

"It doesn't sound like it makes you happy," I said.

Garren shrugged. "Sometimes things are what they are," he said. He took a bite of his tuna salad sandwich. "I have a good client list, and I keep myself busy." It was obvious to me his heart wasn't in what he was doing. Beckett stood and returned to the counter. "Is there something going on between you?" Garren asked in a whisper, his gaze following Beckett.

"Come on. He's my client."

"You keep looking at each other. Even now, he's at the counter and watching you as he waits in line. You know Claude has rules of conduct for his agents."

"Is that why you asked me to lunch today? You were worried that I might have been seeing one of my clients? Or did you want to see if I was interested…?" Garren rolled his eyes, but he didn't deny what I'd said. "You're acting jealous."

"I am not," Garren argued, but the heat I would have expected if I were wrong was missing. The argument was perfunctory. But I let it drop. There was nothing to be gained by fighting with him. "I was hoping we could be friends." He smiled more warmly than I expected.

"Sure," I agreed. I didn't trust him, but "keep your friends close and your enemies closer" came to mind.

"I don't have anyone in my life at the moment and…."

So he wanted to be *that* kind of friend. I was surprised. When I'd accused him of being jealous, I thought he was interested in Beckett, but he was interested in me for some reason.

"Are you seeing someone?" Garren asked.

I sighed. I wasn't sure how to answer that question. "Not really," I answered honestly. I wondered why I was hesitating. It had to be the fact that I knew the question that was looming, and it wasn't one I wanted to answer.

"Would you like to go out sometime?" Garren asked.

"Do you really think that's a good idea?" It was the only response I could come up with. The thought of going out with Garren wasn't totally repugnant. He was a nice-looking guy and all. But I knew in my heart that he wasn't boyfriend material, not for me. "I think we could do something as friends if you like. I have an extra ticket for tomorrow night, if you'd like to go to the play." It was the kind thing to do, but I could see Garren wasn't particularly pleased with my answer. Once Beckett returned to the table, Garren dropped the topic of conversation.

Garren got a phone call as we were finishing. He answered, listened for a second, and grew slightly pale. "I need to get back to the office. I'll talk to you later." He hurried away. I glanced up as he left and smiled over at Beckett.

"Do you get a lot of tickets?" he asked.

"Sometimes. I seem to be a hot ticket right now, for whatever reason, so tickets are coming my way." I wondered if that was Beckett's way of hinting that he'd like to go. "I have an extra ticket for Saturday. It's an off-off-Broadway thing, and I'm not sure what it will be like, but if you'd like to go, you're welcome." My phone beeped. As I read the message, I smiled and relayed it to Beckett. "The contract has been received. Rehearsals begin at eight on Monday, but they want you there at seven for initial measurements for costumes."

"Great. I guess I need to give my notice at the grocery store."

"Yes, you do. There's no way you'll be able to do both." I put my phone away and looked seriously across the table.

"I'll do that, and yeah… I'd like to go to the theater with you. Is it a dress-up affair?"

"I like to dress for the theater. It's part of the magic and makes it an occasion." I'd found that making a big thing of a simple occasion made it memorable and special. "If you want to meet for dinner, we could do that too."

"Sure," Beckett agreed slowly. I could almost see him trying to figure out if he had enough money. "Should I meet at your place at six?"

"Great." I couldn't stop a smile. Yeah, this wasn't a date—at least I didn't think it was a date—but I wasn't going to worry about it at that moment. Though if we did some after-date things that got my heart racing and involved contact with his skin, I wasn't going to say no. "I need to get back to the office, and I'm sure you have things to do. I'll be in touch if anything changes, and you can call me if you need anything."

Beckett nodded. "I will."

I motioned toward the door. "One more thing. I'm going to sound like a real stick-in-the-mud." I pulled open the door, held it for him, and then followed him outside. "You're an artist, and believe it or not, success is going to come your way. And when it does, it will seem like you're on the top of the world, and you'll feel like it's never going to end." Beckett was listening, but I could tell he was already tuning out. "Pay attention. This is for your own good. Our agency is full of people who made it big and now can't get a job playing a dogcatcher. One day you're up and the next you're down. All I'm saying is, make sure that you save some in the good times to get you through the bad times. You landed a great job that's going to last two months. There will be other parts, but it could take time. Be sure to put something aside." I smiled at him. "Before you say anything, I know I'm being preachy, and you can ignore me if you want. But this is a tough business, and you need to be prepared and tougher than it is." We started walking down the street. "You hear stories about guys like Nicolas Cage and think that isn't going to happen to you."

"Don't worry. I have my head on straight when it comes to money."

I breathed a sigh of relief. "Good. Because Gloria—she's one of the most successful agents in town—she could tell you stories that would make your long locks look like Don King."

"Okay." Beckett chuckled. "I get the picture."

"Good. When I got into this business, I promised myself I'd do what I could to try to keep people away from the traps." I bumped his shoulder, and it was like nudging a brick wall. "You know you could at least *act* like you aren't as big as a house."

Beckett pretended to stumble away. "How was that?"

"Too little, too late," I quipped. "Anyway, I was about to say that you are going to love working with Kendall Monroe. He's a really nice guy, and apparently so is his partner."

"He's gay? I didn't know."

"His partner is Johnny Harker."

Beckett stopped walking and stared at me, openmouthed. "He's amazing."

"And apparently Johnny has been working on a theatrical version of his novel, *Love's Brush with Death*. It's very hush-hush, which means everyone knows it's happening, but no one has seen any details."

We arrived at my building, and I escorted him inside and up into the agency. He stepped into the office he'd been using and gathered his things, then joined me in my office.

"I have so many things I have to get done," I said. "But I'll call you if I hear anything more, and I'll see you on Saturday. You did great, and you're going to be a huge success." I wanted to move closer to him. I was tempted to repeat what had happened the other night. Beckett closed the door and came around the desk.

"The other night I had too much to drink and I...." I figured I needed to try to explain my behavior.

Beckett's eyes darkened. "I didn't. I knew exactly what I was doing." He tugged me up by the lapels and kissed me, taking possession of my mouth with lips tasting of mint and man, the perfect combination for seduction as far as I was concerned. My head spun and I moaned under my breath. Beckett deepened the kiss for just a few seconds and then backed away, leaving me breathless. "That was just so you'd know where I stood. What happens next is up to you."

I whimpered as Beckett moved to the door, pausing with his hand on it. My legs were shaking, and I was hard as hell in my pants. I shouldn't want this, and I sure as hell shouldn't be thinking about Saturday night and what he and I might get up to after the play.

"I'll see you Saturday." Beckett yanked the door open, and I sank back in my chair. I wanted him; there was no doubt about it. Now I had to decide which part of me was going to win the battle going on between the caution in my head and the urge to follow Beckett out of the office and down the street until we reached his apartment and, after going inside, staying there for three fucking days. If desire was heightened by anticipation, then I was about to explode.

I took a deep breath to get myself under control before picking up the phone to make a call. I did nothing but hold the damn phone. With my heart still pounding in my ears, I could hear little else. I had to get this under control before Saturday night. That was all there was to it. What I ached for didn't matter: Beckett was a client, and that had to come first. If I told myself that enough times, I might just believe it.

CHAPTER 5—LUST

FRIDAY NIGHT at the theater with Garren was exactly as I would have expected it to be... if it was a scene from a Stephen King novel. We'd eventually agreed to go as friends. I met him at the theater, and we went in together and sat next to each other as the halfway-decent play unfolded on stage. It wasn't a train wreck. I could admit that much. The train wreck happened in the audience, when Garren couldn't sit still for more than five minutes. When he said he'd lost his passion for the theater, he hadn't been kidding. I'd seen six-year-olds watch Shakespeare with a longer attention span. At intermission, he was obviously not having a good time, and I quietly told him that if he wanted to excuse himself, that was fine. After all, I was here to see the performance of an actor playing a secondary character who was supposed to be pivotal in the second act.

"Are you kidding me? This whole thing is a piece of crap," Garren said too loudly, and I shook my head, glaring at him.

"I'm sorry you think so," I said. I watched him stride toward the exit. Before he reached it, he wheeled around on his heels and strode back.

"Are you really going to stay? We could go back to my place for something a lot more fun than this." Garren pasted a smile on his lips that he probably thought was alluring, but it had all the sincerity and warmth of a Mayan death mask.

"I really need to see the second half. Just go on. I'll see you on Monday. It's not a problem, and I'm sorry you aren't enjoying yourself." I wasn't sure what else to say. But Garren wouldn't take no for an answer. He threw his arms in the air, knocking into a woman passing close to him. She bumped into the man next to her, spilling the drinks she was carrying all over him. Garren glared at the mess he'd made for two seconds, but then he must have figured he'd caused enough damage because he made a hasty exit from the theater.

I was appalled at the scene and thankful that everyone followed Garren with their eyes and their wrath, leaving me out of it. The man's clothes were blotted, and the woman was given fresh drinks, while I wished the floor would open up and swallow me. On top of all that, the person I was there to see was the worst in the entire company. Once the evening was over, I was happy to go back to my apartment and replay every detail to Val while he laughed like a loon as we both unwound over late-night cocktails. I hoped Saturday night would turn out better.

I STOOD in front of my closet nook on Saturday night with Val sitting on my bed, a Cosmo in hand.

"Are you really going to dress up in a tux to go out? He's going to think it's a date."

I turned as Val sipped from his glass.

"Now, if you're hoping it's a date and aren't sure if he thinks it's a date, then by all means wear the tux," Val said. "If he shows up in a monkey suit as well, then you'll know for sure."

I took my shirt off its hanger and pulled it on, holding out my arms so Val could help me with my cuff links. "Don't look all put out. If you're going to sit there, you can be useful." He threaded the cuff links, and I worked the studs on the shirt before putting on the bow tie and then making sure the seams were straight. The cummerbund was next, followed by the jacket.

"So, are you hoping it's a date?" Val asked.

"I don't know what the hell I'm hoping for, if you want to know the truth. He's kissed me twice, and both times my brain stopped working." I pulled on my jacket. "What time is Rod picking you up?"

"Half an hour," Val answered, bounding off the bed after downing the last of the cocktail. "I need to go upstairs and get ready myself, but I dare say I'm not going to look anywhere near as good as you do in my ensemble for the evening. But then I'm really going for *out of* my outfit, if you know what I mean."

"I thought you said you were giving up your slutty ways with Rod." I checked that I looked just right and closed the closet door.

"Nope. I only put them on hold. I haven't decided how long the hold is going to last, or how much I'm going to make him work to bring that about." Val giggled. "I hope he's willing to try. Rod is hot, and I'd sure like to see what he's got under the hood."

I met Val's gaze. "Don't make him sound like a car or something. He's a guy, and please go into this with your eyes on something other than his zipper."

"Ha-ha," Val chided as he walked to the door. "Just have fun tonight, and for goodness sake, do something I'd do. And if you do decide this is a date, let him know."

"I'm not too sure how much I've forgiven him for all that stuff from high school."

Val put his hands on his hips and stalked to where I stood. "Don't give me any of that Scarlett O'Hara crap. You don't stop talking about him for more than three minutes at a time, and I bet when you're in the same room, your eyes are glued to him tighter than Greg Louganis's Speedo. Just have fun and don't worry about it. If something happens, then it does. I mean, the past is the past. You can't outrun it because it's always behind you, but that doesn't mean you have to let it dictate your future."

"Okay, Dear Abby, I think it's time for you to go get ready. Beckett is going to be here soon, and so is Rod. We're going to dinner and then the theater. I'll call you if I need anything, and you do the same."

"Oh, please. Don't be a nervous Nellie. I'll be fine. We're just going out for dinner, and then he said we're going to watch a movie or something." Val pulled open the door. "Have fun." He closed it behind him, and I anxiously checked that I looked all right yet again. Finally the buzzer sounded, and I let Beckett inside the front door. He was wearing his new tuxedo, so apparently, at least according to Val, this was a date. I hoped like hell Val was right, because Beckett was black and white sex on a stick, and damned if I wasn't starving. I was also beyond grateful that my pants and coat hid just how hungry I was.

He strode up to me, and I stepped back into the apartment. Beckett approached and pulled me to him, kissing me hard and possessively. "You look really good."

I swallowed. "So do you," I rasped. It was all the volume I could muster. "I made a reservation at a French restaurant close to the theater." I was tempted to ax the plans for the evening and pretend it was Christmas so I could open my presents—my big gift being the one standing in front of me. But I had a job to do.

"All right. But just so you know, I do intend to have dessert tonight." Beckett lightly ran his fingers behind my ears, sending little jolts of excitement running through me. "And I sometimes like to play with my food," he whispered in a deep, rumbly voice. "So let's go to dinner and see the play so we can get to the main event of the night."

Oh God. I was painfully hard, and my ability to think was flying out the window. His fingertips making those tiny circles on my skin and his heady scent were nearly overpowering. I had to step back and take a slow deep breath or the evening was going to end quickly and in my bed. "We should go." I was damn lucky to be able to make a sound. Beckett nodded, stepping outside. I pulled the door closed and locked everything before following. Rod passed us in a pair of jeans and a T-shirt. I wondered for two seconds what kind of evening he had planned dressed like that, but then Beckett hailed a cab, and soon we were inside and on our way to the restaurant.

The food was outstanding, which only added to the excitement that sizzled all through dinner. I could barely taste the arugula salad or the beef Bourguignon without thinking of other things I could be putting in my mouth. During dessert, I kept wondering what it would be like to lick the chocolate mousse off certain interesting parts of Beckett's anatomy. After we were through, I managed to keep my wandering mind in line long enough to get us into a cab and down to the small theater located in the basement of a restaurant. I had been expecting a theatrical performance, so I was wide-eyed when we were escorted to our seats by a beautifully coiffed creature in red sequins and some of the highest heels I had ever seen.

"Is this a drag show?" Beckett asked, leaning close.

"It seems so," I told him with a smile.

"Have you been to one of these before?"

I shook my head. When a waitress, all six-foot-two of her, came to the table, we placed our orders. "Just have fun with it." Last night had been a disaster, and tonight had all the makings of a repeat. I was relieved when Beckett nodded, a half smile on his face. "Excuse me," I said to our server when she returned. "I need a little help. I was asked to come tonight to see Damon. But I'm afraid I'm not going to know which performer that is. I'm a theatrical agent, and...."

"Honey," she said in a voice deeper than mine, "we're not supposed to lift the skirt, so to speak."

"I understand. But how can I consider if I'd like to represent him when I'm not sure which of you lovely ladies I'm to be watching?" I smiled and glanced at Beckett, who had a half-goofy grin cocking his lips.

"Maybe if you gave me this hunk of man for an hour or two, I could be persuaded to reveal my secrets."

"Sweet thing," Beckett began. "That's a lovely offer, but the handsome man in the tuxedo is all mine tonight."

"What about later?" She batted impossibly long and sparkly lashes.

"I think I have everything I need with him," Beckett said, and my eyes widened in surprise. I smiled at him and then turned to the server.

"I really am an agent, and Damon asked me to be here, so please let me know who can help me." I wasn't pushy, but I was becoming a little annoyed. I understood maintaining character, but good customer service was also very important.

She smiled with her apple-red lips and leaned close. Her strong perfume, mixed with a touch of sweat, invaded my space. "You want to watch for Tulane Highway. But if you would, be sure to keep an eye out for Penny Candy too." I got another flurry of batted eyelashes, and then she scooted over to another table.

Beckett and I sipped our drinks. "I really wasn't expecting this kind of evening," I commented quietly. This was a theater, and even though the space was cramped and the ceiling a little low, the walls were bright, and the energy in the room seemed positive. Beckett shrugged and watched the various people as they gathered and milled. The room was set up with seats with tiny tables between each pair for drinks. There wasn't a lot of room to move around, but that was fine. I liked the feel of the place.

Soon the servers disappeared. The lights dimmed, and two men, Penny Candy's brothers, Eye Candy and Peppermint Stick, came out from either side of the stage in G-strings, flanking the enormous mistress of ceremonies. The girls were introduced and the show began.

We were thoroughly entertained, laughed until we cried, and then laughed some more. It had been a long time since I had been so thoroughly engrossed in the antics onstage. The singing was live and the performers were great. Tulane Highway definitely had talent, and Penny Candy could belt long enough and high enough to make Liza jealous. When the lights came up, the room burst into applause once again. The girls came out from backstage and mingled with the crowd. I took the program I'd been given and made a few notes before folding it and placing it in my jacket pocket.

"Did you enjoy the show?" Penny Candy asked, and I pulled a card from my pocket and placed it in her hand.

"Yes. Call me and we'll talk. You have real talent and stage presence as well as a voice. I think we can work together." That got me a huge smile, and she pulled over a lady I recognized as Tulane Highway. I gave her a card as well and thanked her for the tickets. "Midweek would be best to contact me."

"You're serious?" Damon/Tulane asked.

"Yes," I answered, watching as their gazes shifted to Beckett and then back to me. I had to agree with both of them. Words weren't necessary with the way they were both trying to eye-fuck Beckett. He was enough to distract Mother Teresa. "Good night." I smiled, and to my relief, Beckett threaded his arm through mine and we made our way to the exit.

"Would you like to get another drink?" Beckett asked when we reached the restaurant level.

"Yes. But I have the mixings at the house, and I think we'll be more comfortable there." After all, he'd promised that I was dessert, and I was looking forward to that. Beckett paused at the door, turning to me, and I saw the almost feral heat in his eyes. He hadn't forgotten, and I got the idea that if I'd have said yes, he might have reminded me of his intentions right there in the middle of the crowd. As it was, my dick remembered and was standing tall at that very moment, screaming that it remembered Beckett's promise very well and was more than interested in taking him up on it.

We left and I flagged down a cab on a Saturday night only by the grace of God. Another man raced forward to try to jump in it, the rude bastard, but Beckett growled at him and he backed away. Beckett held the door, and I got inside. Beckett followed as I gave the driver the address. Cabs weren't something I normally used. I generally rode the subway in the city or walked, but in a tuxedo, I didn't intend to do either.

I watched out the window, intensely aware of Beckett next to me as each turn had me either leaning into him or him into me. It was an intense dance that lasted all the way through town, through traffic, stoplights, and honking horns. By the time the driver pulled up in front of my building, I swear I was ready to explode. The entire interior of the taxi smelled of Beckett. I paid the driver and climbed out, then hurried to get up the steps, keys in my hand. I unlocked the front door as well as the one to my apartment and let Beckett inside. I closed the door and took off my jacket, laying it on the bed with the cummerbund and tie. I actually sighed as I loosened my collar.

"Let me make you a drink," I said, taking a step toward the kitchen.

Beckett stopped me with a single touch. "I think you should hang up your jacket and put the rest away. Now," he added firmly. I swallowed and opened my tiny closet, fumbling to put my jacket on a hanger and take care of the rest. By the time I'd turned around, Beckett's jacket, tie, and cummerbund were off, and he was opening his shirt.

Acres of rich, honey-olive skin were on display, hinting at plates for pecs with a belly that had a line that led to his navel and then branched off toward places that teased my fevered imagination. Beckett let his shirt hang open tantalizingly and stepped forward, undoing the studs that held my shirt closed. He didn't stop until they were all undone. Beckett tugged the tails out of my pants before pushing the white fabric aside. "Damn," he breathed.

"I know it's a long way from 'Gaydie Paydie,'" I whispered.

"We're both a long way from who we were then," Beckett whispered. "I'm not the same person I was then. But I have to tell you, if this is Gaydie Paydie, then bring it on."

I expected him to kiss me, but he wrapped his arms around my waist, pulling our hips together. I closed my eyes, waiting, my fevered imagination trying to anticipate what was next.

I groaned loud and long when he closed his lips around one of my nipples, sucking and licking in heated ecstasy. My arms hung to the sides as he tightened his grip, sucking harder as he moved across my chest to the other nipple. It was likely I was going to have a trail of light marks on my skin in the morning, but I didn't give a damn. Not when what he was doing felt so unbelievable.

"Take off your shirt," Beckett growled, deep and rumbly. I somehow managed to get my cuffs over my hands and the shirt flung over a chair as Beckett sucked along my collarbone and then up my neck. When the fabric left my hands, he captured my lips with his and I was a goner.

Beckett pressed me back with just the barest hint of additional pressure on my lips. No hands, no pushing, just his lips, and a deep moan that told me exactly what he wanted. The mattress bumped the back of my legs, and I fell back, bringing Beckett along with me.

"Oh God, yes," I whispered as his weight pressed onto me. Chest to chest, lips to lips, I clutched him to keep from flying apart. My brain had no idea what to concentrate on—the kiss, the way his rock-hard chest pressed to mine, or those damned magic fingers that had worked their way into my pants to tease my ass.

"I want you out of these," Beckett whispered as he backed away. He loomed over me, eyes the color of the night sky. "You have one minute to get them off or I'll yank them away." Beckett tugged off his shirt, and it joined mine off to the side. I gasped at the stunning work of art that was his body. I'd already seen him naked in the gym, but that was like accidentally copping a feel, kind of dirty and guilt-ridden. Now the perfection that was Beckett's body was on offer, and I had no intention of turning it down.

I scrambled, kicking off my shoes and shimmying out of my pants. I did find it hard to concentrate on what I was doing once Beckett stepped out of his pants, still in black briefs that strained mightily against their contents and might lose the battle within seconds. I was about to shuck my boxers when Beckett leaned over me and grabbed the waistband. The tearing sound was nearly deafening. The protest died on my lips when Beckett's briefs gave up the ghost. He kicked them off and stood in front of me in all his masculine glory. My lips went dry as he climbed on the bed, straddling me. I cupped Beckett's ass, drawing him closer, guiding his cock to my greedy lips before opening wide and swallowing as much of him as I possibly could.

"Jesus Christ!" Beckett swore. I hummed around his dick, feeling him come apart right in front of me. Few things in my life had been as exciting or fucking awesome as the way Beckett went to pieces right there with my lips around his cock. That I could do that to him was the biggest erotic boost I had ever had. Beckett quaked, shaking the bed slightly as salty sweetness filled my mouth.

I loved the way a thick cock felt sliding on my tongue, and Beckett tasted and filled me in the most amazing way. I slowed my movements, gripping Beckett with my lips as I grabbed the most amazingly hard ass in the history of the world. Beckett stretched above me, and I lifted my gaze upward over rippling muscles and glistening skin to his open mouth and glassy eyes. His chest heaved up and down, muscles clenching, and I sucked harder.

Beckett stroked the top of my head and pulled away. "It's too soon," he rasped through deep breaths. I whimpered softly as he stepped off the bed, staring fire through me. I wondered for a split second if I'd done something wrong.

"Beckett," I whispered in confusion.

He leaned over me, his chest hovering above mine, lips close enough to feel his breath. "Just be patient," he whispered, barely touching my lips with his. He took my hands in his and gently lifted them over my head. I wasn't sure how I felt about being held like this, but those reservations flew from my head when he sucked one of my nipples and then licked a trail of heat down my chest and belly, ending up where my cock bounced against my belly.

I gasped when Beckett sucked me into his mouth. My eyes crossed and I lifted my hips off the bed, needing more of the wet heat that surrounded me. I shook from head to toe. Then I realized Beckett's lips were gone. I opened my eyes and saw Beckett staring at me. He'd let go of my hands.

"What happened?" he asked.

I swallowed and must have turned beet red. "I've never—"

"What?"

"—had that happen before?" I should have simply said nothing.

Beckett gasped. "You've never had a blowjob before?"

I shook my head and wanted to die.

"What kind of selfish pricks have you been dating?" Beckett asked sharply.

I shrugged and swallowed.

"You know that giving is just as wonderful as receiving, and that you deserve both, right?"

"I'm Gaydie Paydie, remember?"

Beckett huffed. "You were never Gaydie Paydie, and you aren't now. Yes, we were all asses in school and called each other names, but please don't let that define you. I was a jerk in school because I was one person then and I hope I'm not him any longer. You aren't either."

"You can say that now," I retorted, stronger than I intended. "You weren't the one who was the butt of everyone's jokes."

"No, I wasn't. And yes, I know you were, but we were the ones who were wrong." Beckett placed a hand on my chest, the heat searing into me. "You deserve to receive just as much pleasure as you give, and you deserve better than the selfish assholes you've been with."

That was easy for him to say, but hard as hell for me to believe.

Beckett took my hands in his once again, but this time he stroked the backs with his thumbs. "I want you to relax and close your eyes."

I wasn't sure I could. My heart raced, and not for the reason I hoped it would at a time like this. My own reaction confused me.

"Just close your eyes."

I did, but I reopened them two times before holding them closed.

Beckett lightly stroked my chest and then over my belly. The excitement that had abated began to return. "That's it," he whispered and continued stroking, almost petting me as he closed his lips around my cock.

God, that felt good—fucking awesome, really—and he took me deeper, sucking harder. I knew how to give good head, but getting it bordered on overwhelming. Beckett slowly moved his lips up and down my cock. As he did, he wrapped his arms around my legs. I lifted them to my chest and he took me deep. I gasped and gripped the bedding, afraid I was going to rip the covers.

When he pulled away, I thought I'd die of disappointment. But within seconds he wrapped a hand around my cock, stroking as he sucked and licked my balls. "Fuck, I love that you shave," Beckett whispered huskily. "That is hot." He licked, sucked, and stroked until I had a difficult time pulling in air.

When he paused, I breathed deeply, able to get enough oxygen once again. But damn if he didn't steal my breath when he released my balls and swirled his tongue around my opening. Sex for me usually involved oral sex, me giving, and anal sex, me getting fucked. It did not... or had not, involved me getting rimmed until I couldn't see straight. The heat, Beckett's fingers and tongue, teasing, licking, sucking, probing—all of it combined and built into sensory overload. I clamped my eyes closed and just gave myself over to him. I had no choice. He made me feel more alive than I ever had before, and now that I'd experienced that, I needed it to last forever.

"I'm going to come," I warned. Control over my own body was slipping away fast. Beckett pulled away, all sensation ceasing. The shock left me bereft. Then Beckett kissed me, hard, possessively.

"What do you want?"

I opened my mouth, but not a single sound came out. That was a question I had been asked so rarely in my life I didn't know how to answer it. What the hell did I want? "Fuck me" finally passed my lips. I pointed to the stand beside the bed, and Beckett leaned over me. I smiled and brought my mouth to the nipple that was right there, licking and sucking his musky, slightly salty skin. God, he tasted good. Beckett paused in his movement. I wound my arms around his broad chest, splaying my hands across his powerfully muscular back. Ripples of restrained power danced under my palms. Beckett was strong; there was no doubt about that. I had seen him in action at the gym, and one look was enough to tell anyone that. But the way he moaned and his gentle touch belied a warm heart that I never would have known he had if I hadn't given him a chance.

Beckett stretched and the drawer slid open. "I can't think when you do that," Beckett whimpered.

"Thinking is overrated," I quipped and then continued sucking his now pebbled nipple.

He managed to get what he needed and banged the drawer closed. I chuckled as I continued licking and sucking at his chest. What could be hotter than making a big guy like him forget what he was thinking?

Beckett pulled away, kneeling on the bed, most likely intending to get himself ready. I flipped onto my belly and sucked him deep in one fluid movement.

"You need to warn me," he said, the bed shaking slightly as I sucked him hard as a rock. Beckett slid his hands down my back and over my butt. I hummed softly around his fat cock as a spit-wet finger teased at my opening before sinking into me. I pressed my ass upward to give him better access, sucking him while he fucked me with first one and then two of his thick fingers. "Like that?"

"Uh-huh," I hummed, cock in my mouth, fingers in my ass. When Beckett rubbed over my happy button, I groaned and wriggled my rear, hoping for more.

Beckett pulled away. "Sweetheart, I'm going to lose it in a few seconds." Beckett ripped open the condom packet and rolled it onto his cock with shaking hands. I flipped onto my back, and Beckett parted and lifted my legs with his knees, then leaned over me, kissing my blowjob-spit-slicked lips as he pressed into me. The stretch and burn cleared my sex-clouded head for about half a minute. Then he sank deeper, and I moaned softly as he filled me.

"Jesus, you're huge."

"You know just how big, since you had me down your throat."

"Yeah, well...."

He slowed and let me adjust before pressing deeper until his hips slapped against my ass.

"Man...," I breathed.

"I know. You feel amazing and look even hotter laid out for me." Beckett inhaled deeply, and I went right along with him, quickly matching him breath for breath. Then he began to move, slow little movements at first that gradually worked their way up to fast, powerful snaps of his hips that rocked the bed and my world at the same time.

"Beckett...."

"I know. You're amazing."

I wasn't so sure about that, but this was hardly the time to argue. "Don't you dare stop!" I could already feel the pressure and pleasure building inside. Beckett slowed down, and I smacked his chest with my palm. I had never hit anyone or even gotten my butt slapped during sex before, but dammit, I was going out of my mind. He slowed some more, and I did it again.

"Getting demanding and pushy."

"Need to come."

"You will when I let you." He batted my hand away from my cock.

"Now."

"No." Beckett thrust deeper, shaking my body, my cock bouncing against my belly. That little sensation sent a thrill running through me. "Not until I'm ready." His chest glistened with sweat. He arched his back, sending his massive chest forward, adding additional power. Beckett looked like a god: shoulders for days, chest muscles that rippled, arms deeply corded, anchoring him above me. This was the erotic vision of a lifetime, and I had no idea how much longer I could keep from careening over the edge of climactic oblivion, sensation or not.

Beckett stopped, breathing deeply. I did the same, uncrossing my eyes and blinking away the tears that filled them. He leaned forward, kissing me hard. "Right now, for tonight, you're mine, and I want to show you just how good it can be. This is all for you."

"But...."

Beckett touched a finger to my lips, and I quieted. "Whatever kind of selfish ass you've been with before, I want you to put that out of your mind." Beckett's cock jumped inside me, rubbing lightly over and past my prostate.

"Oh God." My cock bobbed against my stomach, bouncing and getting a little sensation, but not... quite... enough. I was getting desperate, and when Beckett kissed me again, he moved almost painfully slowly. I desperately wanted more.

"Not yet," Beckett warned before pulling entirely out of my body and then sliding back deep in a single movement.

"Damn. Like that."

Beckett did it again, pounding into me. The rhythmic movement filled the room with the steady slap, slap of flesh on flesh. I couldn't resist any longer. I reached for my cock, thanking all the gods that Beckett didn't bat my hand away again. I closed my fingers around my shaft and stroked hard, just the way I liked it. I relished the warmth and excitement that instantly built in my balls and at the base of my spine. Within two strokes, the pressure built into heat that started in my legs, raced up my back, and bloomed into a release of epic proportions.

Thinking was not a possibility, and neither was talking. I came hard, shooting on my chest and belly, and I might have hit the headboard. Hell, with the way I felt, Greenland was a distinct possibility. Beckett had stilled and I wondered if he'd come as well until he began moving slowly once again, picking up the pace. I expected to feel lethargic, but that didn't happen. My entire attention focused on Beckett and the continuation of our journey to ecstasy.

"Give it to me," I demanded. "Yeah." Holding on to the bedding, I let Beckett take me on a ride. My cock refused to wake, but I didn't care in the least.

A boom echoed through my apartment, and I instantly gasped, feeling the sound deep inside. Beckett stilled completely. Instantly the mood in the room shifted. He slipped from inside me, the bubble of ecstatic happiness instantly popping around us. Heavy footsteps sounded from above

"What the hell was that?" Beckett asked.

"I don't know, but...." That came from Val's apartment. I listened intently, but heard nothing more. "My friend lives upstairs," I said quietly.

Beckett moved away from the bed, already pulling off the condom.

"I'm sorry." I knew something was wrong. In all the time I'd lived here I'd never heard anything like that from Val's place. But I still wanted to die.

Beckett dropped the condom in the trash can, frustration rolling off him. Not that I could blame him for a second. "You need to check on your friend," Beckett said.

I nodded. "Will you still be here?" I expected him to say he'd leave. I was waiting to hear that as Beckett began yanking on his clothes in a "building on fire" hurry. I pulled on my pants and stepped into my shoes while I pulled my shirt over my head and took the few steps to the door.

I pulled the door open and hurried into the hallway, listening for Beckett's answer to my question even as I headed for the stairs. What I hadn't expected was for Beckett to be right behind me.

I heard Val's door bang open, and Rod appeared at the head of the stairs, red-faced, jaw set, eyes burning with rage. I managed to get out of his way, but Beckett stood across the stairs. Rod barreled past me, but he came to a halt when he reached the brick wall that was Beckett.

"Let me the fuck past!" Rod roared.

"You aren't going anywhere." Beckett crossed his arms over his chest, glaring back. I turned and continued up the stairs as fast as I could and burst into Val's apartment. The main room looked the same as it always did. The bedroom door stood open, and when I reached it, I stopped. Val lay in the center of the bed, which now stood askew, his eyes filled with tears, face red. He was naked, which I'd seen before, but the bruises blooming on his wrists and shoulders had me gasping in alarm.

"Val." I made my legs work and strode to the bed. I didn't want to hurt him, so I refrained from touching him. "Honey, can you talk to me?"

"No," Val whined, and then he covered his face with his bruised hands. The only indication I had that he was crying was the way his shoulders shook.

"Do you want me to call an ambulance?" I asked. Val shook his head. "Are you in pain? Did he really hurt you?" I checked around the bed to make sure he wasn't bleeding. I breathed a small sigh of relief. "I mean, do you think anything is broken?"

"No," he whispered and then choked. "He... he...."

I leaned closer and carefully hugged him. Val melted into my arms.

"Payton, I have this guy out here," Beckett called.

Val shivered. "Don't let him near me," he gasped and clutched me harder. "I never want to see him again."

"Should we call the police? I'll stay here with you if you want." Seeing my positive, outgoing friend reduced to tears broke my heart.

"No. Just get him out of here," Val managed to say.

"Okay. I'll be gone for just a few seconds." I went to move away, and Val held me tighter.

"Don't go."

"Okay." I turned toward the door. "Beckett," I called.

"Yeah."

"Let him go."

"You sure?" Beckett asked.

I turned to Val, who nodded.

"Yes."

Heavy footsteps faded. A few minutes later Beckett stuck his head into the room. "I found your keys and locked the door for you," he said to me. He left and I turned back to Val, letting him cry it out. Beckett returned with a glass of water and handed it to Val. I smiled at him, both surprised that he hadn't run for the hills and that he was being so kind.

"He's gone," Beckett whispered. I met his gaze over Val's shoulder. "Take him to the bathroom and help him clean up."

I nodded. I guided Val off the cockeyed bed and helped him to his feet. He let me help him to the bathroom. I grabbed a towel and used it to cover him, then I got a cool cloth and pressed it to the back of his neck. Val sighed and seemed to settle down a little. "It's going to be all right," I murmured.

"No, it's not." He gulped air, and I gently stroked his back to try to keep him from hyperventilating.

"Yes, it is. I know it hurts now, but it will be all right. I'm here for you, and Beckett is out there watching out front to make sure he doesn't try to come back."

"Why do I attract losers? I thought he was nice. He held the door for me when we went to dinner, and we walked for a while, talking. I thought he was nice. It wasn't until we were naked that he turned into this demanding asshole, and when I said no, he only pushed harder." Val gasped and sniffed. "Thank God the bed broke, because the noise scared him, and he jumped away and couldn't get dressed fast enough."

"How many times did he hit you?"

"I don't know. Once or twice. He grabbed me hard more than once, and...."

I knew in my heart that things would have escalated and that Val had probably gotten very lucky, considering. I kept that to myself and comforted him as best I could.

"He didn't force himself on me—at least, it didn't get that far."

I listened and continued rubbing his back to calm him. "It will be all right. I promise you that." I wished some guys knew how to take no for an answer.

"I know," Val agreed meekly. "I feel so stupid. I should have done what I said I was going to do. I wasn't going to bring him back here. Dinner and maybe go somewhere fun, but then say good night. That was the plan, and stupid me, always thinking with the little head, let my dick take the lead… again." He banged his hand on the counter.

"Stop that. You had no way of knowing he was some kind of freak." I had never particularly liked Rod, for whatever reason. Of course, now I pictured him with the eyes of a snake and the forehead of a Neanderthal.

"I'm so dumb."

"No. You were taken advantage of. That doesn't mean you're dumb."

The bathroom door cracked open and Beckett stuck his arm inside, holding a pair of my shorts and a T-shirt. Bless his heart. He hadn't wanted to go through Val's drawers so he'd gone downstairs to mine. I took the clothes and tried to remember if I had anything in those drawers that I didn't want him to see. "Put these on," I told Val gently.

He stood and turned away, mechanically pulling on the shirt and shorts. I took Val's hand and opened the door.

Beckett sat on the edge of the now-righted bed. "I was able to fix where the side rail had come out."

"So it isn't broken?" Val asked.

"No. It hadn't been hooked properly in the first place. I checked the others, and they're fine."

Val stared at the bed, then pulled off the spread and grabbed a pillow, hugging it to his chest as he left the room. I got the feeling the bed was not going to get any further use tonight, and possibly not for a while. In the living room, Val plopped down on the sofa, still hugging the pillow, and stared at the blank television screen. Beckett caught my eye and shrugged. I did the same, having no idea what to do or say.

"Vodka," Val said flatly.

"No."

"I need to forget."

I shook my head, stepping into his field of vision. "You need to calm yourself and relax. You're safe. Alcohol is only going to make things worse, and you aren't going to forget."

Val glared at me. "Why are you wearing tuxedo pants and an open tuxedo shirt?" He turned to Beckett. "Both of you."

"Nice segue," I quipped.

Val rolled his eyes. "Were you two…? You were, and I messed that up too." Val pressed his face to the pillow and kept it that way for a while. "You should just go back to what you were doing. I'll be fine here." The television screen behind me seemed to take on renewed interest as Val's eyes lost focus once again.

"What we should do is make sure you're all right," I said. "Is there any coffee or tea in the kitchen? Preferably decaf."

"You can look," Val answered.

Beckett got busy heating water and found what looked like herbal tea of some sort.

I sat next to Val, pulling him to me. "You know this is over and you never have to see him again."

"What if I do?"

"You won't," Beckett said firmly. I turned, catching Beckett's gaze over the couch. "Before I let him go, I scared the living shit out of him. Let's just say I doubt he made it home without soiling something."

"You didn't come in," I said.

"Didn't need to. I heard the fear in Val's voice in the hall. This place isn't that big, and I made sure that guy knew he wasn't welcome any longer." Beckett cracked his knuckles. "He also left with a wrist that's going to look an awful lot like yours."

"Good. I wish you'd beaten the shit out of him, but that will do. Thank you." Val managed a tiny upward curve to his lips.

The kettle whistled, and Beckett made the tea and brought over mugs that he handed to both of us. Then he sat in the chair farthest away. "What you need is to drink your tea and then try to get some rest. He's gone and isn't coming back, I can guarantee that. When we were on our way up, he was running like a scared piece-of-shit bunny."

"Thanks," Val said before sipping from the mug and then setting it aside. "You're both lifesavers." Val rested his head on my shoulder, and I put my mug aside, hugging him. "You know, this guy is a real keeper." If Val could say something like that, he must have been feeling a little more like himself.

"I hope so," I said.

"Go on back down to your place. I'll be okay, I promise. I need to take a shower to make sure I don't smell like him, and then I'm going to do as Beckett said and try to sleep."

"If you're sure," I told Val. He nodded. "But you have to promise me you aren't going to hit the hard stuff once we're gone." Val didn't answer me. "I'm not going to go until you make me a pinkie-swear friendship promise."

"What's that?" Beckett asked.

Val sighed. "We used to do it as kids, and it means that if I promise and break it that we'll no longer be friends, and that he'd get to give me five noogies and a swirlie."

"Six noogies, but you get the idea." I held up my pinkie.

He took it, rolling his eyes. "I promise I won't have any alcohol. I'll just lie down after I finish my tea." We clamped pinkies. "You're a swine for making me do this."

"Yeah, yeah. It's for your own good and you know it."

"What if I didn't agree?"

"We were going to clean out the apartment." There was no way I was going to let Val drown his fear. "I'd get a box and lug every bottle out of here with me."

93

"Bitch," Val countered, with none of his usual catty mirth. His heart didn't seem to be in it. That told me as much about how he felt as anything else. "Now go on. I'll be fine."

I wasn't so sure he was telling the truth, but I gave him a hug and walked to the door.

Beckett leaned to Val, whispering something, and Val nodded once. Then Beckett followed me out of the apartment, down the stairs, and into my place.

"God, I'm so sorry about all this." I pulled my shirt closed, self-conscious now that I had a chance to think about the fact that my shirt had been hanging open the whole time we'd been at Val's.

"It wasn't your fault," Beckett said. "Your friend needed you, and you charged up there like an avenging angel."

I shrugged. "Let me get your things." I turned, and a huge arm slid around my waist.

Turning back, I was met by gentle eyes and a soft crook to his lips. "Do you really want me to go?"

"I figured you'd want to after all that." I ran a hand down my face. "Two disasters in as many days," I murmured.

"What happened yesterday?" Beckett half demanded. "You never said anything about it."

"I went to the theater with Garren. He said he wanted to be friends, and I had tickets. It's no big deal. He didn't like the play and made a scene in the lobby. It was pretty rude on his part. Then after I thought he'd stormed off, he hurried back. The whole thing was stupid."

"Did he think it was a date?" Beckett asked with a gruffness to his voice that I wasn't sure if I liked or not. Though the gruff part had my dick already thinking there might be more fun in the future. Well, that and the way he rested his hand just above my ass.

"I don't know…. I guess."

"What did you do to make him think that? Isn't he just a coworker?"

I stepped back, pulling away from his arm. "I didn't do anything. He said he wanted to be friends. But he wanted more. I turned him down, and he stormed off."

"You must have done something to…."

I felt cold, and I let my eyes reflect it. "You need to leave now."

"I didn't mean you did it on purpose," Beckett clarified as I pointed toward the door. He had an expression just like the one he used to have in high school, like he knew something you didn't. In that second, I knew what I had hated about him then. That loathing was back, and just like that, it was as though the last few weeks hadn't happened.

"Yeah, right, because nothing happens that isn't under Beckett's control, so somehow, some way, the feelings of a coworker I was being nice to and friendly with because I was trying to do a better job are my fault." I was angry enough to spit nails, and I wanted him to get out of my sight so badly I was shaking. "You're a condescending ass."

Beckett rolled his eyes toward the ceiling, bobbing his head slightly back and forth. "Probably."

I stopped. "So you admit you're an ass."

"I'll admit to being condescending. Having a great ass is all God's work."

"I said you were an ass, not that you had a great one." Though I could hardly argue the point. I wasn't sure whether to try to wring his neck or laugh. I ended up shaking my head in total confusion. "I can't believe you admitted that."

"What, that I was condescending? Come on. When have you known me not to feel superior? How do you think I made it through high school after I was outed? I was suddenly…?"

"Me," I answered for him dryly.

"I was going to say the object of ridicule." He glared at me, and I wondered what the hell he was getting at. I was getting very close to telling him to leave again. But frankly, I wondered where he was going with this, so I crossed my arms over my chest, tilted my head to the side, and waited to see how much deeper he dug himself into this hole. "I did it by thinking the way I always had. You think I felt any different than you most of the time? I was scared shitless that people would find out about me, and then everyone did. So I pretended I was still better than all of them, and fuck if it didn't work, because everyone pretty much came around."

"Well, lucky you. Too bad your luck isn't holding tonight. That attitude is only going to get you shown the door, and while you're at it, you can stop the wounded jealousy routine too."

"You have to admit, it sounded for a second like you'd gone out with two guys in two days. Not bad, in general, but it feels shitty if one of them is me." Beckett shook his head slightly. "You know what I mean." I loved the hint of frustration in his voice. "So, okay, I'm sorry for acting jealous. I have no right to."

"Okay," I agreed in my most put-upon manner.

"But…." He stepped closer. "I still hate the idea of you seeing someone else. That's just for the record."

"You're really pulling that crap after what happened tonight?" A shiver ran up my spine, like I'd just crossed paths with a ghost.

Beckett paled. "I'd never do that, and I think you know it." The thing was, I believed I did. Beckett once again came closer. "If you want me to go, I will. Just say the word. I'll leave right now, and we can just be old friends and maintain our business relationship." His scent drifted around me, gently tugging me in. "Or we can pick up where we left off, and I can slip out of these clothes, unpeel your lithe body from what you're wearing, and fill your hot, tight little ass with my cock." He came even closer, his voice becoming softer so I had to lean in to hear him. "And ride you until you scream for me."

Fuck. I watched, shaking, as he shrugged off his shirt, then tossed it over the chair. The pants were next, his cock bobbing in front of him. He kicked off his shoes and stood naked in front of me. I probably would have drooled if I could have made my throat work. "Yeah," I managed to say, and Beckett pulled off my shirt and pressed me back onto the bed. He did exactly what he said he would, and against all my better judgment, I let him have his way with me. My own release from before had dried on my belly and shirt. Beckett licked it away as he trailed his tongue up my belly, chest, and neck in search of my lips. He ended up there eventually, and I was so glad he seemed directionally challenged.

When Beckett entered me for the second time, I did scream, against his lips. After the initial sound, he kissed it away, swallowing my cries as he made good on his promise, over and over again until I was so exhausted I couldn't remember a thing and fell into sweet oblivion.

CHAPTER 6—LETTING GO

I TOOK Val to the theater with me on Sunday to take his mind off what had happened and to keep an eye on him. "You haven't said more than ten words all afternoon," I told him gently.

Val shrugged, but he didn't argue with me. I didn't blame him for being upset, but it still worried me that the Val I loved seemed to be hidden away. "I just want to curl into a ball," he said.

"You can't," I whispered to him when the play blessedly reached intermission. I was about to ask him if he wanted to leave, but he sat back in his red theater seat and stared up at the ceiling. I did the same, admiring its evocatively cracked plaster. The theater had been built on a Moorish theme, but it had degraded into Moroccan maudlin over the years.

"I know." Val rolled his head to face me. "What gets me is that I liked him. I've dated assholes before, but this guy got in under my bullshit radar. I keep wondering what would happen if someone does it again." He shivered, and I hoped to hell it was the overenthusiastic air-conditioning.

"Dating sucks sometimes."

"Says the guy who's made the catch of the year."

I rolled my eyes. "Please."

"Think about it. He could have run when all that went down last night, but he didn't. He helped and scared the crap out of Rod." Val sniffed. "He brought me water and tea and made sure I was safe, so if you don't want him, can I see if he's interested?" Val wiped his eyes and sighed. "Why bother? He only has eyes for you… and other things, if what I heard in the middle of the night was any indication."

"It's lust, and he thinks I'm fun. I like my time with him, but I doubt it will ever be more for him, and I won't have my heart shattered again by some drop-dead gorgeous guy who only wants a little fun."

Val humphed. "Well, all I want is a nice guy who's hot. You got one, and…." He shook his head.

"Let's not talk about Beckett or Rod. We're out at the theater, so how about we enjoy this lackluster play and see if we can find a diamond in the rough somewhere." I smiled, and he nodded, some of the gloom lifting as the lights dimmed.

"Fine," he whispered. "But when are you going to see him again?"

"Thursday," I answered with a smile. It was nice seeing a little of the Val I loved beginning to peek through once again. He was in there beneath the now-livid bruises. They would fade over time, and so would the hurt and doubt, but things like that sometimes left scars that weren't visible, possibly deep ones, and all I could hope was that they would fade as well as the outward signs.

THE SECOND act was only slightly less dreadful than the first. The actors weren't bad, but whoever's brother-in-law had written the play should have been taken out and shot for crimes against drama. The best part was when the actress playing the villain, dressed in a long cape with a train, had the hero on his knees, begging. Fortunately for the audience, he knelt on the edge of her cape and when she walked away… yoink. Just like a cartoon. We all laughed, hard. Thankfully she wasn't injured, but the incident clearly unsettled her. It was a shame. If she'd remained in character, it could have been powerful. Instead, it was pathetic, but very funny. She did finish the play, but the spark she'd had was gone.

When the lights came up, we left our seats. "Is that the guy from your office?" Val asked. I looked where he pointed and saw Garren leaving the theater. He saw me and hurried away. "What's up with him?"

"We all scout for potential talent. There's nothing to stop him." However, the look he flashed left me cold and I moved closer to Val.

"There's something wrong with that guy," Val whispered. I felt him shaking. "Let's get out of here. I don't want him anywhere near me."

"I know he's a little off, but the guy isn't dangerous. I work with him every day." I gently took Val's arm and coaxed him toward the exit nonetheless. As we approached the doors, Garren caught up with us.

"Did you see anything interesting?" Garren asked. He shifted his gaze to Val. "Three different men in as many days." He raised his eyebrows, and I seethed inside.

"Val is a friend, and we were out as friends, nothing more." I guided Val away. He was getting more upset, his arm shaking, and I hoped he wasn't having a panic attack. "We have a reservation in a few minutes," I lied, but I didn't care in the least. I had to get Val outside.

He sucked air hard as soon as we were on the street. The crowd moved around us. Once we got to the corner, I hailed a cab and got Val inside. After giving the driver the address, I pulled the door closed and the car sped into traffic.

"Sorry. There's something about that guy...."

"It's all right." I watched out the windows as we cruised the streets of Manhattan. Well, as much as possible in a cab fighting all the traffic signals. Val calmed down, and by the time we reached our building, he was breathing normally and his eyes were a lot less saucerlike.

My phone rang as we got out of the cab. I fumbled with it as I paid the driver. "Hello," I answered absently, the phone between my shoulder and ear as I closed the cab door.

"Is everything all right?" It was Beckett. Even his phone voice sent warmth through me. This had to stop, because I could easily get used to his voice and the thrill of his simplest touch. I knew in my heart that Beckett would wake up eventually, some more interesting guy would come along, and that would be it.

"Yes. I took Val to the theater. He got a little upset, but we're fine." I followed Val inside and we went upstairs. Val unlocked the door and peered inside before stepping into the apartment.

"I wanted to make sure the guy from last night hadn't shown up again."

"He hasn't, but Garren was at the theater acting weird."

"What did he do?"

"Nothing. Just acted like an ass." I wasn't going to go into the details. "Val is still pretty shaken up. I was hoping an afternoon out would be good for him. I think he had a good time, but he's skittish, and that's not like him."

"You do realize it's going to take him more than a few hours to get over what happened, right?" Beckett said. "He was attacked in his own home by someone he liked. That's enough to upset anyone. Now he doesn't feel safe, and the one place he should has been violated."

"Yeah. I know you're right." I followed Val into the apartment.

"There's no need to talk about me like I'm not here," Val sniped as I closed the door.

"I'm not. Beckett was wondering how you were doing."

"That's nice. Tell him I'm fine and that I want to be alone for a while." He plopped down on the sofa and pulled a light blanket over himself, holding it like a shield. "I'm just going to watch television and heat something up for dinner. Go on and have some fun. I'm not going anywhere."

"Can I call you back?" I asked Beckett, and I ended the call after he agreed. "Are you sure you're okay?" I asked Val after setting my phone on the table.

"Yes…. No…." Val lifted the blanket until it was up under his chin, leaving only his head and a shock of blond hair visible. "I don't know what's going to happen. I feel like shit, and I don't want to go anywhere or see anyone. The theater was nice, but then I saw that Garren guy and I wanted to run home, except what if Rod was waiting for me?"

"You know, you aren't alone," I told him, sitting on the edge of the sofa against his legs.

"What are you going to do? Move in here with me?" Val shook his head. "Somehow I have to figure out how I can go back to work tomorrow and be surrounded by people." He gasped. "What if Rod shows up there?" He shook like a leaf.

"Tell your boss and he'll take care of it. You have people to support you."

"Maybe," Val admitted, calming enough that the sofa didn't shake any longer. "You should go now and let me be for a while. I'm only going to watch television."

"I let you have a drink with lunch, but remember your promise," I cautioned. "You know I'd get way too much pleasure out of giving you those noogies." Val actually smiled for a second. "Call me if you need anything. I'm working on some scheduling for the week, so I'll be home."

"Go out, do something," Val told me. "At least call Beckett back and arrange to stay in, have fun." The light in Val's eyes lasted only a few seconds. I stood and decided to take him at his word.

"I'll go as long as you promise to call in a few hours." I hugged him before leaving the apartment. I pulled the door closed and heard Val throwing the locks as I started descending to my place. I returned Beckett's call once I got inside. He asked about coming over, and I agreed to order a pizza. It seemed I wouldn't get much work done, but that was okay. I figured I'd have as much fun with Beckett as I could while it lasted.

The door buzzer sounded, and I peered out the door, expecting it to be either the pizza man or Beckett. Instead I saw red when I realized Rod was standing outside the door. I had no intention of letting him in. I wondered why he was ringing my door in the first place. Maybe he'd rung them all to see if anyone would let him in.

I grabbed my phone. "Beckett," I said as I closed the apartment door. "Rod is out in front of the building, and he's going to get in if anyone opens the door."

"I'm on my way," Beckett told me.

"Val will freak out if he sees him." I opened my door once again. Rod peered through the glass, and I shook my head, letting him see the phone. I didn't much care who he thought I was calling. I wanted him to go away.

"I'm approaching the building. Stay inside." He disconnected, and of course I got pissed at him for telling me what to do. So I did the opposite. Once Rod stepped away from the door, I went up to the glass to see what was happening.

"I said to stay there," Beckett called when I opened the front door.

"Bossy much?" I shifted my most withering gaze from Beckett to Rod. "How dare you come here!" I demanded. "After what you did last night. I spent the day trying to calm him down. He's scared of his own shadow, and that's because of you, and you have the cojones to show up here again?"

"I didn't realize what was happening. We went out and I remember asking him to go dancing. Then the next thing I know, the room is spinning. We sat down, and Val asked me back to his place. I felt weird, and by the time I got to his apartment, I...." He looked down at the ground. "I don't know what happened after that. I remember being with him and then Beckett here throwing me out, but I don't know why."

"That's bullshit if I ever heard it." I crossed my arms over my chest and turned to Beckett to see if he was buying any of this. To my surprise, he seemed to be, which only fueled my anger further.

"Is Val okay?" Rod asked.

"No. You left a trail of bruises all over him. He slept on his sofa last night because he can't sleep in his own bed right now. So I suggest you go away."

"I think I was drugged or something. You can ask anyone who knows me—I'm not a violent guy. I was in the Army for a while, and I swear all I keep remembering about last night was being back in combat. It's so strange, like the evening was ripped out of some memory, and I was transported back there and then home again."

"Look. You better give Val some room. He's hurting right now," Beckett said. "Pay will tell Val what you said when he thinks he'll be able to handle it. Until then, you need to leave him alone."

"I only came because I wanted to make sure he was okay. I had flashbacks and things after I came home from Iraq, but I thought they were under control. I guess not... and last night felt like one." Rod sighed. "If nothing else, please tell him he didn't do anything wrong and that the things I remember about being with him were very nice." Rod turned away and slowly shuffled down the sidewalk, head down.

"Damn, that's one hell of a thing."

I took a step down until I was chest to chest with Beckett. "First off, if you buy that shit, you're a fool. You saw what happened, and I'm not going to tell Val anything."

"Don't you think Val has a right to know? At least tell him the part where Rod said that none of what happened was Val's fault. It might help him feel better. Secondly, I told you to stay inside. What if he hadn't been that docile?"

"Let's get something straight, Mr. Huntington." I poked my finger to his chest. "Just because you're as big as a brick outhouse, that doesn't mean you get to tell me what to do."

"Even if it's for your own protection?"

"I'll decide what I need. I might not be as huge or as intimidating as you are, but I can take care of myself." I shook with fury.

Beckett took my finger, and I braced for him to get angry. Instead, he took my hand in his other one and held it gently. "Sometimes you can be so prickly." He brought my fingers to his lips. "I don't want you to get hurt, and I was only protecting you. There's no need to get all twisted up." He then sucked on one finger and then another. "One of the benefits of being as big as I am is that I rarely get into an actual fight. Other guys are intimidated and back off."

"What are you doing?" I asked as he sucked two of my fingers between his lips.

"Giving you a preview of what could happen if you'd let go of that anger of yours." He chuckled softly. "Are you always so full of piss and vinegar?"

"Yeah. It comes with having nothing and trying to make something of myself. You have to be willing to work hard and not take no for an answer."

A throat cleared from behind us. "I have a pizza...." The guy was clearly trying not to look.

"For Payton?" I asked.

"Yes."

I stepped away and ran inside to get my wallet. When I came out, Beckett held the box and the deliveryman was nowhere to be seen.

"I took care of it, and he scurried off like a scared rabbit."

"You can be a little much for some people," I told him, shaking my head when he scowled. "Use it to your advantage."

"When I do, you yell at me."

"Only when you use it on me. Intimidating assholes and others is okay. Just don't try to use your size with me. Not that it will work. I know you well enough now."

Beckett humphed. I unlocked the front door and we went inside.

"Are you going to tell Val about Rod?" Beckett asked.

"What about him?" Val asked as he came down the stairs.

I groaned. "He was here, but we got rid of him," I said.

"Did he say anything?" Val came down the rest of the stairs, and I closed the apartment door after motioning him inside.

"Yes, and I don't want to talk about it with you now. He did say to tell you that what happened wasn't your fault and that you didn't do anything wrong."

"Oh...." Val said. "Then why did he act like that?"

"I don't know. He claimed it was a combination of someone slipping him something and post-traumatic stress. I told him he needed to leave you alone."

"For what it's worth, I think he was telling the truth," Beckett said, and I growled. "Pay isn't convinced."

"He said he came back to make sure you were okay because he couldn't remember what happened very well. He said that for part of the night, he thought he was back in battle," I explained.

"Oh," Val said, a little more brightly than I would have expected. "That makes me feel better, a little."

"You do?"

"Well, yeah. I kept thinking everything was my fault somehow. It wasn't, I know that, but I still kept wondering." I glared at him. "That doesn't mean I'm going to go out with him again, but if that's what happened, then I hope Rod gets the help he needs." Val looked longingly at the pizza box, so I pulled out some plates while they sat down on the sofa. I got some iced tea and brought in glasses. Then we ate. Val inhaled the food. I was grateful I wasn't too hungry because Val seemed ravenous and finished off the last of the pizza.

"I should go," he said sheepishly. "Now that I've eaten your dinner."

"It's fine. I'm glad you were hungry." It was good to see him doing something other than mope. "Go on and get some rest."

"Do you think I should talk to Rod?" Val asked.

"You can if you want to," Beckett answered. "But I think Pay is right. Take some time and make sure you're okay. He has his issues, and you already brought them home once. You don't need to do it again."

Val stood. "I just thought I'd found a nice guy." He sighed and moved to the door. "You're right, though. It's best if I let this go."

"I don't know what's best for you, and neither does Beckett." I stood and hugged Val tightly. "You're my best friend, and I don't want anything to happen to you."

"I know. I want you safe too." Val looked over at Beckett. "I think you'll be more than safe with him around." Val leered, and I was glad to see some of his humor coming back. "Just keep it a little quieter than last night." He patted my cheek. "You have quite a set of lungs on you."

I groaned as Val left the apartment, closing the door behind him. "I was surprised you called."

"Why?"

"Well, I keep wondering what you must think after last night and then today. My life is becoming much more dramatic than I ever expected."

"With what you do for a living, I'd think you'd enjoy some drama every now and then." He grinned, and I knew what was coming next. I wasn't disappointed. "Do you know what I like most about this place?" Beckett prowled closer. "Nothing is very far from your bed."

"You have a one-track mind."

"Are you complaining?" Beckett tugged me to him.

"I need to get all this cleaned up." I pulled away and gathered the trash and plates, then took them to the kitchen. "Don't look at me that way. I know that once you get down to action, we aren't going to get anything else done all evening." Hell, it wasn't likely I would even be able to think. "And you need to be up early because of your rehearsals, so I think we should get to bed early, and the thought of cleaning up later isn't appealing." I rinsed the dishes, keeping an eye on Beckett as he hovered impatiently nearby. It was fun as I slowed my pace and saw him shifting his weight from foot to foot, sighing every few minutes. "Any task worth doing is worth doing right."

"Is that so?" Beckett strode over, and I squeaked like a kid when he lifted me off my feet and into his arms. "Well, then, I'm making an exemplary task of taking you to bed," he told me, his voice a deep rumble. I had a smartass retort forming on my lips, but he kissed it away. Then he laid me on the bed. "You listen this time. I need to lock the door and turn out the lights. You are to be naked by the time I get back." He kissed me again and then pressed his lips to my ear. "I'm going to suck you so hard and long your brains will turn to mush. Then I'm going to eat your ass until you beg me to fuck you into tomorrow. If you have any problem with that plan, you best tell me now."

I swallowed and shook my head. When he stepped away, I scrambled to get my clothes off, like he said. The lights clicked off as I removed the last of them, the city light from between the curtains providing just enough to see by. The city had taken some getting used to—the constant background noise that permeated everything and the constant light that shone everywhere. I was glad of the light at that moment, because I got to see Beckett remove his shirt and then his pants. "Turn around," I whispered, and Beckett faced the wall. I sat on the edge of the bed and tugged him closer before sliding my hands down his rippling back and over the curve of his incredible, perfect bubble ass. He turned slowly back to face me, his hip passing under my hands. When he faced forward, his cock pointed directly at me, and I wasted no time.

Beckett groaned deep in his throat as I sucked him, threading his hands into my hair. I loved how I could make him whimper and groan, like I had power over him. He bent forward, his cock slipping from my lips. Then he held my cheeks gently in his hands and kissed me, pressing me back on the bed. I went where his lips and mouth guided me. No words were needed. Beckett had an amazing ability to communicate what he wanted without making a sound. Once I rested my head on the pillow, Beckett pulled back and met my gaze with his fiery one before breaking contact and sliding down my quivering body. I wanted to watch, but I ended up closing my eyes, the sensation and excitement just too much.

He took my cock into wet heat, sucking me just the way he'd said he would, deep and hard. He had this thing he did, keeping my cock at an angle so his lips added more pressure, and damn if that didn't have me panting within seconds. When I was shaking hard with the need to come, trying to stave it off, Beckett pulled back and lifted my legs. My cock was still jumping when he scraped his tongue over my opening. I whimpered as he went deep. He'd promised me the rimming of my life, and that's what he gave me.

He gave me time to catch my breath as he rolled on the condom, and then he took it away again when he stretched me open and entered me with amazingly controlled force. I never wanted this to end.

"Did I keep my promise?" Beckett whispered against my lips, buried deep inside me, unmoving at the moment.

"You always do," I answered breathily. I realized it was true. He did what he said he was going to do, and he kept promises he made.

"Just remember that," he added as he slowly began moving again.

"Jesus!"

"Don't scream to him."

"Beck!" I cried, and he shifted the angle, sending waves of ecstasy racing through me.

"That's better. Tell me what you want. Let me know what I mean to you."

I wrapped my arms around his neck and kissed him as the power of his thrusts sent ripples through me that I transferred back to him. Time had no meaning when we were together like this. Minutes or millennia were the same. He played me like a fine instrument, up and down, rest to crescendo, in a way that could have gone on forever, but my body had other ideas, and when Beckett stroked me, I came within seconds, Beckett following right behind.

I couldn't think straight. Thank God Beckett held me all through it, grounding me while my mind flew in a million amazing directions. Then it settled and I was back in Beckett's arms.

A single tear escaped my eye, and I felt Beckett catch it with his thumb.

"Why?" he whispered.

I shook my head, blinking away the remainder that threatened. "It's nothing." At least it was nothing I could do anything about. I held him closer, knowing deep in my heart what was coming and what I was going to have to do. I hugged Beckett tighter and gasped when he slipped from inside me. I wanted him to stay there as long as possible, but nothing, no matter how good, lasted forever. Beckett climbed off the bed and shuffled to the bathroom. I heard water run, and when he returned, he handed me a warm cloth. I wiped my skin and dried it with the towel, blinking as Beckett returned to the bathroom and then came back.

"Is what's between us real to you?" Beckett asked once he'd settled in bed again, tugging me to him.

"I don't know." That was a bald-faced lie and I knew it. There was something real between us. No one had ever made me feel the way he did. Just knowing he was on his way over had sent a rush of excitement through me, and it wasn't just because he was amazing in bed. The excitement came from seeing him and being with him. That was what made the time we spent together special.

"You don't?" Beckett said, and my heart clenched at the slight break in his voice. "You don't know what I feel for you."

"Beckett, I'm sorry. I never should have let things go as far as they did. I'm your agent and you're my client." Damn, this was so much harder than I ever imagined. But I'd be a fool to let this go on between us. "If Claude finds out that we've been seeing each other like this, I'll lose my job."

Beckett released his hold on me and rolled onto his back. "So this was just some kind of game for you? I hurt you in high school, so you tried to see if you could get back at me?" He sat up quickly.

"No. It was never that." I swallowed around the lump in my throat as I saw the most amazing connection I'd ever had with anyone wither and die right in front of my eyes. "You have an amazing career ahead of you, and I really like my job and want to keep it. I also want to see your career take you everywhere you want and deserve to go. I can't do that if I lose my job."

"I see." Beckett looked at me over his shoulder, and his face caught a stream of light from the window. His eyes were wet.

I couldn't watch any longer or I'd lose my nerve, which was hanging on by a thread at the moment.

"For the record, I think you're so full of shit," he said. "This is all about things that happened years ago, and you know it." He stood and began yanking on his clothes with such force that I swore stitches gave way. "Was there some grand plan to hurt me? To get even for the stupid things I did when we were in school? That was years ago, and I thought you had forgiven me, that we'd moved past all that."

"I have. But maybe you're the one who hasn't moved beyond the past. I can't have a relationship with you, no matter how much I might want to, without losing my job. You have to understand that this is the best thing for both of us." All I could think at the moment was how my heart broke when he turned to me, the despair on his face telling me more than anything else. He cared about me—he might even have loved me given time—but that was clearly over, and I was throwing it all away… had thrown it away.

"I should go. You've said enough for one night, and I need some time to think." Beckett buttoned his shirt and sat in the chair to put on his shoes and socks.

"Don't forget you have your rehearsal tomorrow. It's your first, and you need to be sure you're at the top of your game."

"That's all you really care about, isn't it?" Beckett stood and stepped closer. "You know I would have given up any part, hell, I would have given up the theater altogether and never set foot on a stage again if you'd asked me. I love the theater more than anything. Well, I thought I did until I met you again."

110

I tugged the sheet around me, feeling exposed and more than a little cold, wanting to sink through the floor under Beckett's withering gaze. Suddenly what I'd been so sure of a few minutes ago seemed shaky. I couldn't take back what I'd said, but I wanted to more than anything. No one had ever been willing to give up what they loved for me, and I hadn't been willing to do the same for him.

"I'll see you later, and don't worry, I know what's truly important to you. I won't let any of this get in my way. Rehearsal will go well, and I'll do whatever they ask." Beckett unlocked the apartment door and pulled it open, light flooding in from the hall. "I'll see you—" I heard that break in his voice, and he said nothing more.

"Beck, I—"

But the door closed before I could finish what I wanted to say.

I stared at the door, pulling the pillow to my chest. He was gone, and yet with each breath, I got more and more of his scent. It was on the pillow I was holding, and I placed my face to it, filling my nose with all I had left of Beckett.

I threw the pillow back on the bed, wondering what I'd just done. Beckett was gone from my personal life, and I felt as empty as I could ever remember. My head told me I'd done the right thing, but my heart—I knew it would ache for a long time. I was a fool and now I was a lonely one. I lay back down, pulling the covers over me, but the bed was too big and empty. Beckett was gone, and I had been the one to push him away. I wanted to talk to Val, but he was hurting as well, and I couldn't dump my stupidity on him. So I stared up at the ceiling, determined not to cry like a stupid little kid. It didn't work. I lay there, tears running from my eyes, knowing I'd let an amazing person slip through my fingers.

Eventually I fell asleep and dreamed of Beck. We were at the show, laughing at the drag queens' antics. Then, suddenly, the scene morphed and we were back at my apartment, Beckett forceful and gentle at the same time, taking me to heights that left me breathless. I woke with a start, throbbingly hard. But that lasted only a few minutes. I remembered that the bed was empty and Beckett was gone. I had him now only in my dreams—and it was my own fault. I had pushed him away, for all the right reasons, I believed, but still… he was gone. I should have known I couldn't have it all. Everything had a price, and being involved with a client was not something my job allowed. I told myself it was better this happened now rather than later, when things were even more serious and the separation more painful. Still, it seemed painful enough already.

THE FOLLOWING morning, I dragged myself into the office. I hadn't slept well at all. I kept thinking about Beckett. Mostly I wondered how I had let him get under my skin, but I had and he'd touched my heart. I had to put on a brave face and get on with my work. It was what kept me going, so I went right to my office, glad I'd gotten in early.

"You had some weekend," Garren said, sticking his head into my office.

"What do you want?"

"I keep wondering what the guy you were with on Saturday would think of your date on Sunday? I know nothing happened when we were out, but the Sunday guy was quite cute."

"You're such a pig," I hissed softly. "Why are you acting like this, anyway? We went out as colleagues, and you made a scene. Why do you care who I go out with or why?"

Garren ignored my question. "What I want to know is if you're involved with one of your clients. And judging by the rings under your eyes, I'd say you were having a great deal of fun with someone."

"Things with Beckett are strictly professional." I could say that truthfully now, even if it made my heart ache just to say the words. "Now, I have work to do, and you probably do as well." I turned away and checked the list of phone calls I needed to make. Garren left, thankfully, and I got to work.

I managed to contact Tulane Highway—Damon—and through him Penny Candy, aka Carl, and set up appointments for them to come in that afternoon.

The staff meeting was scheduled at noon, and Claude had arranged for lunch. I took my chair at the meeting, and when my turn came, Claude asked me about new prospects. "You've been on quite a roll, young man," he said with a smile.

"I attended a number of performances over the weekend. One was ghastly, but the performer I was there to see was very good. She's coming in tomorrow morning. I believe I can get her proper work that will showcase her talents. Last night's play was all right, but the prospect was wooden. On Saturday I saw an amazing show. Two of the performers are coming in this afternoon." I couldn't help smiling. "Penny Candy and Tulane Highway." I used their stage names on purpose.

"Drag performers," Garren said with a laugh. "We don't represent them."

Claude shot Garren a stony look and then shifted his gaze to me. "Are you sure about this?"

"They're amazing. They don't lip-synch, but perform their own songs. They sing, dance, and act on stage as well as play convincing women. It was an incredible show, and they were the stars. *Kinky Boots* is huge, and so is RuPaul. There are roles for them on television, and if they wish to perform as men, I could get them work that way as well. These are performers, and that's what we represent. I was impressed." I nearly said Beckett and I were impressed, but I swallowed that part. It surprised me how easily that would roll off my tongue. It felt right, but now it was gone.

"I'm not sure," Claude said.

"Through contacts, I could book them into Las Vegas in a heartbeat. As I said, they were great, and with the right representation could go a long way."

"All right. Talk to them," Claude agreed. "We have never represented drag performers, but if they're the real deal, then I want to know about it. Is there anything else?"

"Other than that, I have a full slate of performances this weekend as well. I wonder what will come of that?" I smiled, and Claude grinned.

"You'd go to the theater twice a day if you could, wouldn't you?" Claude asked.

"Of course. I love the theater."

Claude turned to the others. "That's what we're all here for. That's our business. I know we get people parts and help build careers, but it starts with the love of the theater and performing. So I want you all to go at least once a month." He turned to his right. "Even you, Gloria. Spotting new talent is how our business grows. Yes, we sometimes lure talent away from another agency, but then in turn they can be lured away from us. Good work, Payton. Keep up the initiative. I know it takes time to build a clientele. That's why we hire on a stipend for the first year." I nodded my thanks, and Claude turned to the group. "Just so everyone is aware, we will not be hiring anyone to replace Jane at the moment. Each of you has room to expand, and I expect you all to. This is an opportunity for each of you to increase your slice of the pie. So get out there and find new talent." He continued with the rest of the normal business, and I sat back, happy as I could be. Once the meeting was over, I hurried back to my office and picked up my cell. I had actually started to call Beckett.

I sighed. I would have called Val, but he was at work. So instead I smiled to myself and then began making business calls.

"Payton, you need to come to the lobby," Millie said with a grin as she stood in my doorway.

"I take it Penny and Tulane are here."

"Yes, and oh my." I followed her out, and sure enough, they were dressed to the nines.

"Hello," I said, greeting both of them. Penny was a dream in a royal blue gown that flowed like water, and Tulane was in green, showing leg and an amazing body.

"Do you think they would have any tips for me?" Millie asked.

"Honey, if you want, we could give you the works. The whole catastrophe," Tulane said with a gentle smile. "Your husband or boyfriend wouldn't know what hit him when we were done."

Mille giggled, and Claude came to his office door, clearing his throat to get attention.

"Claude, this is Tulane Highway and Penny Candy," I said.

"It's nice to meet both of you." He looked at me as though I'd lost my mind. At least I thought he did until he turned back to them. "I'd like to see your show."

Tulane opened her purse and produced two tickets. "Tell them I sent you and they'll seat you right down front." I had never imagined Claude could blush that deep a shade of red. "You and your wife will be thoroughly entertained."

"I'm sure we will," Claude stammered, and I motioned the ladies toward my office. Claude caught my eye, and I hung back a minute. "Okay. You made your point." I wasn't quite sure what point I'd made, but I was happy he was pleased. I thanked him and met the ladies, escorting them into my office.

"You both made quite an impression," I said as I closed the door.

"It's what we do, darling," Tulane said. "Drag is big and getting bigger."

"I realize that. But the reason you're here is because of your talent. This isn't some drive to get on the drag bandwagon. You both have talent, and plenty of it. The singing, dancing, the whole package. I do have to ask a few questions, though. The talent you both have transcends your clothes and persona."

"I don't understand," Penny said.

"All right. The talent doesn't belong to Tulane and Penny, but to Damon and Carl. Do you want me to only book work for Tulane and Penny? Because I could also get work for Damon and Carl. The gift is there—it shines past the clothes and makeup."

Tulane opened her purse and dabbed her eyes with a tissue. "Thank you."

"Now it's my turn to be confused," I said.

"Tulane is part of me just as much as Damon is. But no one noticed me until Tulane arrived." She dabbed her eyes once again and put the tissue away.

"It's up to both of you. What I'd like to do, if you agree, is have a portfolio created of both sets of looks." Tulane and Penny looked at each other as though they weren't sure. "You don't have to decide right away. Take your time and think about it."

"The thing is, as Damon, I have stage fright. Going in front of people just isn't his thing. But Tulane gives me the courage and freedom to be this fabulous. Once I take off the makeup, I'm nothing special."

Penny nodded in agreement.

"All right, then. I have my answer. That's no problem. I can get you plenty of cabaret work, and I hear that a cast change is possible at *Kinky Boots*. Also, we have some contacts in Las Vegas, so we could get you work there as well as Hollywood. But first I want to help get you publicity here."

"Can you do that?" Penny asked.

"I can certainly try."

"I was thinking of trying out for *Drag Race* next season," Penny said.

I leaned across the desk. "You could do that. But it's a gamble. If you make it to the end, it can help, but if you don't, you can be hurt by it. See, they don't remember what you did well, only where you fell flat. My feeling is to build a career the old-fashioned way, through talent and hard work."

"I'm in," Tulane said.

"Me too," Penny agreed.

"Excellent. How long are you booked currently?"

"We have a few more months, and then the show will change and everyone will have to audition again. That's Jerry the Jerk's sense of humor. He likes to keep everyone on their toes, so no one knows whether they'll be out on the sidewalk every six months. He likes suckups."

"All right. If you sign with me, I will not take anything unless I get you a job. If you like, I'll also negotiate on your behalf with Jerry the Jerk. And I'll see what I can get you." That show wouldn't be the same without either of them, so I figured I could come at him from a position of strength.

Both of them smiled and nodded. "Is it all right if I ask you something?" Penny inquired. "You were at the theater with that hunkalicious man. Is he your boyfriend?"

I tried to suppress a sigh. "He's another client."

"Seemed like more than that to me, and believe me, Penny knows these kind of things. He was looking at you like you were candy and he hadn't eaten in months." Her red lips curled into a smile.

"Well, things are complicated. But he's just a client now, and that's the way it should be." Mixing business with pleasure was a recipe for heartache. I should have known that. It was my fault for getting caught up in the attraction.

"Complicated, schmomplicated. You two looked so good together, and you can pull that 'just a client' thing all you want, but you could barely take your eyes off him during the show. And neither could anyone else. You two were gorgeous together. We all had to compete to hold the audience's attention, and that never happens. So what's the dish?"

"Excuse me?"

Tulane interrupted. "Ignore her. She's always getting her nose in other people's business. It's none of your business who he ki-ki's with, Penny. He's our agent, not one of the men you try to fix up. Penny here thinks she's some sort of drag yenta."

"Well, there's nothing to do. I shouldn't get personally involved with clients, and I let myself get carried away."

Penny tutted lightly. "So you let him go so you could keep your job?" She continued to shake her head. "If you loved the guy—I mean, like, loved him for real with a happy-ever-after and all—then no job is worth giving that up for. Or were you only in lust with him? Because, honey, I could fall in lust with that man in about two seconds flat." Penny fanned herself. "I think I'm halfway there just thinking about it."

"Calm down, missy. Can't you tell he still has a thing for this guy? You don't need to go stepping on other people's toes. Remember the last time you rushed in? You got threatened with a pair of pumps up the ying-yang, and even I know you aren't that kinky."

"All right," I said. They had me chuckling in spite of myself. "It's over."

Penny's expression turned serious. "Your mouth says that, but your eyes say that your heart isn't so sure."

I blinked a few times and took a deep breath. I needed to clear my head, get my thoughts back on the task at hand. "Do you have pictures we can use to put together a portfolio?"

"Goodness yes," Tulane said. "We could plaster your apartment walls with them. We love to have our pictures taken. She and I both have portfolios of a sort, but they're a little more artsy than the average person's."

"This is a serious business," I began, imagining the folios covered in glitter and bedazzled with rhinestones. "And I want potential employers to take you seriously. You're both talented performers, and you deserve to be treated as such. It's part of my job to see that you are, but it's yours as well."

"We are serious," Tulane said, in a much deeper voice than before.

"Good. Then the way you look is important, but so is the way you present yourself. When going to an audition, you should look the part you're going for. And you do. But your professionalism should be beyond reproach. That will impress them as well."

"People expect fabulousness from a drag queen," Penny argued. "It's our job to give them that."

"Yes. In your outfit and makeup, you should always be fabulous." I smiled and opened my desk drawer. "Here is the type of portfolio I put together for my clients. It's simple, clean…."

"Bor-ing," Penny quipped.

"Yes. But any producer knows what it is and…." I opened the cover. "…it lets the pictures inside speak for themselves." I hadn't realized I'd pulled one of Beckett's. The amazing close-up of him in his tuxedo, those eyes blazing from the picture, startled me. I stared at his lips for a few seconds, licking my own as I remembered his deep, possessive kisses that I'd felt to my toes.

"You all right, honey?" Tulane asked gently.

"Yes, sorry." I adjusted myself in my chair, glad I was behind a desk. My heart wasn't the only part of me holding out hope. "What I thought I'd do is have these made up for both of you, but instead of a blank cover, I'll get ones with a photo frame cover and insert the best photograph as the cover. Again, they'll be simple. Well, simpler, and it will let you and your images speak for themselves."

"All right," Tulane said. She stood up with all the grace of a dancer. "I'll put myself and my career in your hands."

"Me too," Penny said.

"One more question. Will you accept work as a duo?" I asked.

"Excuse me?" they asked in unison.

"I'm thinking of options. And you look great together." It was only a suggestion, and from the looks I got, not one that they'd contemplated.

"We each have our own act already," Penny said.

"Let the man speak," Tulane snipped at Penny as she sat back down. "What did you have in mind?" Penny sat as well, looking none too happy.

"Maybe a *Bosom Buddies* type of thing?"

"Or a Fred and Ginger type act?" Tulane asked.

"I get to be Ginger," Penny piped in, holding up her hand.

"They *always* want to be Ginger," Tulane said, overacting and rolling her eyes.

"See, that's exactly it right there. You two have been playing off each other ever since you walked in my office. I'm just saying there could be gold there if you're willing to explore and mine it. I'll sign both of you regardless, but options are always good in this business, and in my opinion you two are amazing and have a world of opportunities."

Both Penny and Tulane fanned themselves. "You are good for our egos, sweetheart," Penny said with an affected Southern drawl.

I smiled. "Now we'll get down to the ordinary details. I'll go over the standard agency contract. If you agree to the terms, then I'll have final agreements drawn up and sent over to you for review and signature. Or you can come in, if you like. Either one works. Once that's done, I'll get busy on your behalf."

We spent the next half hour going over details and getting information. It would have been quicker, but my phone kept ringing and I had to put out a fire with a client who had forgotten his audition time. I apologized when my phone rang again. I answered it quickly and then got back to Penny and Tulane.

"Don't you worry, if your phone wasn't ringing, we'd be nervous," Tulane said.

We finished our business, and they got up to leave.

"When we sign the agreement, I need you to send me the details of your current contracts so I can see what I can do for you," I said.

"I brought mine with me, and Penny says hers is the same." Tulane pulled a small packet from her purse and handed it to me. I opened it right away and was astonished at the amount they were being paid.

"This will never do," I told them as I did some quick math in my head.

"Why do you think we call him Jerry the Jerk?" Tulane said

"Jerkoff is more like it. The cheap son of a...," Penny added.

"I'll send the agreement over quickly and then get to work."

We shook hands, and I walked them out of the office, past Millie's desk, where Tulane handed her a scrap of paper.

"If you're really interested in some fashion or makeup tips, give me a call. You have an interesting face, and we could do a lot with it." She smiled, and Millie giggled, taking the paper as though it were the Holy Grail. Millie always looked extremely professional, but nothing more. They left the office, and I returned to mine, making phone calls and arranging for the contracts to be put together and sent out.

Caught up and exhausted, I left the office a little early, forwarding my office phone to my cell. I intended to take the subway home, but it was a nice day, so I decided to take a walk and ended up going through the theater district. I loved this part of town, with the lights and marquees. They hinted at the magic and excitement to be had within. Without thinking, my feet carried me to the theater where Beckett was rehearsing, and I stopped in at the box office.

"Good afternoon, I'm Payton Gowan, the agent for one of the actors in the play being rehearsed. I was wondering if rehearsals were still going on?"

"They are," the man in the box office said, without giving anything else away.

"I wanted to check how my client was doing," I prompted, and he finally nodded and came out of the box office and led me through to the theater. I whispered a thank-you and sat down in the back row. He returned to the office, and I watched Beckett as he stood on stage in jeans and a T-shirt. They weren't mic'd, so I couldn't really hear them, but that was fine. I didn't need to. Beckett moved though the scene with ease and without stopping. At the moment he was playing opposite Kendall Monroe, and the two of them were amazing together. I was spellbound by their interaction and the way they played off each other.

When the director asked them to stop, I quietly got up and moved closer. As I did, I heard the pleasure in his voice. "That was exactly what I wanted. In fact, it was better than what I had in mind. Let's go on to the next scene."

All the actors held scripts except Beckett. He had one nearby, but worked without it, acting his lines from the heart as he recited, "But love is more than what can be bought or what you can get. It's about putting someone else above yourself."

I gasped and covered my mouth. My stomach lurched, and I breathed through my mouth to try to calm myself. That single line summed me up in a way that was almost eerie. The scene continued, but I didn't hear much over my heart pounding in my ears. Stopping here had not been a good idea. Beckett was doing wonderfully; he didn't need me.

I got up and quietly walked toward the back of the theater. I heard the stage go silent, but I continued walking. I didn't want to disturb their work.

"Payton, what are you doing here?" Beckett asked quietly from behind me.

"Making a mistake. I just wanted to see how things were going, but it was a bad idea for me to show up."

Beckett looked around, then pulled me out and into the darkened lobby. "That's bullshit and you know it."

I wanted to move into his arms and hold him. I was so close to giving in. "Maybe, but…." I sighed. "I really need to go."

"What are you afraid of?" Beckett demanded. "And don't feed me that line about work again. I didn't buy it last night, and I'm not now. So you tell your boss that I'm your client and that we knew each other in high school. We're dating at the moment, and both of us understand the possible ramifications. Big deal. This isn't Victorian England or something."

"Claude…."

"Isn't going to care, and neither will anyone else, as long as you don't lie about it. So I know there's more to this than your job." Beckett paused and listened. "I need to get back to work."

"Look, Beckett, I'm sorry." God, this hurt like hell. "You know this is for the best. You deserve someone…."

"What? Are you going to be magnanimous and say you aren't good enough for me or some other lame cliché? Please. If you don't want to see me anymore, that's fine, but at least be original." He turned and then paused, looking back. "I can forgive insecurity. We all have that. And I can forgive a mistake, but quoting a bunch of overused 'let him down easy' lines is just being a coward." He scowled. "Maybe Gaydie Paydie isn't as far in your past as you like to think."

"You son of a bitch," I said, forcing the words through my teeth.

"Think about it. In high school it wasn't being gay or even your weight that made you a target. It was your attitude. You made yourself a target by looking like one. And you're doing it again. You were afraid of your own shadow then and you're afraid now." Beckett strode to the theater door, pausing with his hand on the handle. "When you figure out what you want and stop acting like a chickenshit, call me." He pulled open the door and walked inside, letting the door close after him.

I stood shocked into immobility, wondering how he had seen through everything I tried to project to the world. The damnedest thing was that I couldn't say he was wrong, but I was not going to go back in there and tell Beckett he was right and beg for forgiveness, either. And talking to Claude about my love life, or possible love life, wasn't something I could do. I had been with the agency for less than a year. Adding drama and personal-life complications wouldn't help my reputation. Regardless of what Beckett thought, his solution wasn't that simple. As for the rest, Beckett might think he knew everything, but....

I checked my watch, realizing I'd been standing alone in a dark theater lobby, arguing with myself under my breath. Time to go home alone and get on with my life. I left the theater and continued my walk downtown. I had many blocks to go and plenty of time to think about what I truly wanted.

CHAPTER 7—LIGHT

"I STILL can't believe you were dumb enough to push Beckett away without even fighting for him."

"I had to, you know that," I argued.

"Why, because Garren, a weasel and a lowlife, told you that your boss has a thing about agents dating their clients? He may, but you didn't even check with anyone, did you?" Val shivered. "That guy gives me the willies. But what's worse is that you took what he said as gospel, and because you were afraid of whatever consequences, you pushed Beckett away."

I had never thought of that. I cringed. He was right. I had let my own fear take over everything.

Val lifted his glass filled with a pink cocktail to his lips. "In the beginning, I couldn't believe you were giving Beckett the time of day after you told me what he'd done to you. But it turned out he was a really nice guy, and as hot as they come. And to top it off, I think he really liked you, *for you*."

"You make it sound like I have leprosy or something." I took the glass he offered, and we sat down on Val's sofa.

"Nothing like that. But it's hard in a city like this—where everyone has one eye on the guy they're with and the other on the door in case someone better comes along—to find someone who really likes you for the person you are. I think you had that with Beckett, and you gave it up way too easily."

"Great. Now I'm stupid and a fool." I set my glass on the coffee table. "Maybe I should go back to my apartment and just be alone. I'm obviously too stupid to be around other people."

"Stop acting like a drama queen. You made a mistake and let Garren play on your fears. He probably knew your job was important to you and hit a nerve. Now he's interested in you, personally."

"That's creepy."

"No kidding. But he's crappy at his job, as you already know, and you said his heart isn't in theater anymore. So he's trying to get the new guy off his game because you were making him look bad. The other agents have all been there a while, and they are well established. Garren isn't much older than you are, so he's still rather new. Do you know how large a clientele he has?"

"Not really. Though he never seems especially busy, and he isn't out actively hunting for more." I shook my head. "I thought he could have been a friend. Sure, we argued over a client, but he didn't gloat or anything."

"And he got you off your guard." Val took another sip of his drink.

"So what do I do?" I asked hopefully.

Val raised his glass in my direction. "I don't know. I'm not the relationship guru. I have my own issues in that department. At least Rod has stayed away. I don't know if I could take facing him." He drained his glass, and I gently took it from him and set it on the table, giving Val a stern look.

"I know you're still upset about all that. But dealing with it is better than burying it."

Val humphed softly. "This coming from the guy who gave the bum's rush to one of the best men in the city because he wasn't dealing with his own issues."

"That's not fair."

"Bullshit. You're free with your advice, but you don't take it. Look, I know you did something stupid, and I have to ask, do you want Beckett back?"

"Yeah," I said. "It's been four days, and all I do is think about him all the time. I didn't know him that long, and he already worked his way so deep into me that I dream of him every night and wake up shaking, alone, and unhappy."

"Then what are you going to do about it? You saw him on Monday and came home miserable. Since then you've been a pain in the ass. I hope you haven't been like that at work, or your clients are going to hate you."

I shrugged.

"Figure out something. It's time you stopped acting like your entire life is in someone else's hands."

"I don't do that," I protested quickly.

"You do too. You let Claude, Garren, and your job dictate who you can have in your life, to the point that you let Beckett go." He leaned forward. "And just so you know, anyone who can make someone else moan and scream the way Beckett had you going should be held on to with both hands and legs wrapped around his waist. So call him, go over there, talk to him. I don't care what you do, but actually do something besides mope. Frankly, you didn't have the date from hell on Saturday, and you're bringing *me* down."

I threw up my arms. "All right."

"Good, because I did not want to have to tell you to grow a set, but I would." Val snickered. "I'll tell you something else: if you don't tell him how you really feel and quit hiding behind your insecurities, someone else is going to work their way in and it'll be too late."

"I honestly hadn't thought of that."

"Now that's enough of all this maudlin crap. I haven't been to the gym at all this week, and I dare say neither have you. So get your things. We're going to the gym. All this feeling sorry for ourselves only puts on pounds and makes our skin blotchy."

I loved that each day a little more of his sense of humor returned. "Fine." I stood and went to the door. "I'll meet you down at my place in ten minutes and we can head out." Lord knew I could use some time getting my body moving. Maybe I could get Beckett out of my mind for a few minutes.

WHY I'D thought this was a good idea was beyond me. I walked on a treadmill watching a parade of manhood pass in front of me. Some were covered up in sweatpants and T-shirts the way I was, and others wore tiny shorts and shirts that were barely there at all, showing off sculpted bodies. None of them compared to Beckett, and I found that the parade of handsome guys only became points of comparison.

"Stop scowling," Val said from the next treadmill. "Everyone is staying away."

"So? I'm here to exercise, not get lucky in the showers."

"Speak for yourself. Your mug is casting a shadow over this entire area of the gym. Besides, since you're so determined to let Beckett go, you might as well find someone to replace him."

I sighed.

"Just as I thought. You aren't interested in anyone else, and you're determined to make everyone else as unhappy as you are." Val turned away and made a show of ignoring me as he met the gazes of a few of the guys he knew. At the gym, the faces were largely familiar, and I was pleased that Val was getting socially active again. There wasn't much that could keep him down for long, and thankfully the marks on his face were gone. His wrists were still dark, but those bruises too were fading. I wasn't sure how much of Val's bravado was real and how much was him putting up a front, but it was good to see nonetheless.

A large blond man approached Val's treadmill from the other side, getting on and starting the machine. I turned away, but heard the two of them talking softly.

"What happened to your wrists?" the blond asked.

I glanced over and saw Val stumble for a second, then regain his footing.

"A guy I thought was nice got way too rough last weekend. I kicked him to the curb." Val held his head high, and I was proud of him.

"Not into rough stuff?" the blond asked, and Val shook his head. "Good, I'm not either." He leaned a little closer and I couldn't tell what was being said over the whir of the machines, but Val broke into a smile, and I decided to find something else to occupy my attention.

"Hi, Pay."

I turned around and forgot to walk. The machine caught my feet. Somehow I managed to hit the emergency stop button before it threw me off. Beckett steadied me anyway, and I blushed like a total fool. "Hi, Beck." I swallowed hard, not sure what to say.

"This is Eric," he said and stepped back.

A man almost as large as Beckett took a step closer and held out his hand. "It's nice to meet you," I said.

"This is my agent, Payton," Beckett said, and the last strings of my heart broke. Val had been right. Beckett had found someone else already, and I had screwed up what could have been the best thing I'd ever have.

Eric smiled. "He told me he had this awesome agent who got him a great job."

I stifled a cringe. I was not going to take on Beckett's new boyfriend as a client, no matter what. I wanted to get the hell out of there now, but my feet were plastered in place. "Beckett is very talented, and he got the job. I just paved the way."

"Eric is in town for a competition and is using the gym as a base to keep pumped. He and I got to talking, and then I saw you." He reached over and tapped Eric on the shoulder. "He and I competed against each other a few times."

"Beckett won those battles. But I was always the one who got the ladies." Eric grinned, and I breathed a sigh of relief. "He was never interested in them, which was cool, so after the competition, I'd always collect the ladies and have a good time. He's, like, a chick magnet. They love him." Eric smiled and slapped Beckett lightly on the back. "He's a great guy."

I nodded. "That he is." I had messed things up bad, and now I didn't know how to make it right.

"We should get back to work before we cool down too much," Eric said, and Beckett nodded. "It was nice to meet you," Eric said before turning to stride to the weight area. Beckett hung back, his gaze intense.

"Have you had time to think about what happened?" Beckett asked.

I nodded. "I was scared," I admitted. "You were right."

"About your job?" Beckett asked. "You're an excellent agent. You could work for anyone, and now you have clients who will follow you."

"I'd like to think so, but that wasn't it. Not really."

"Then what was it?" Beckett asked.

I shook my head. I didn't want to have this conversation, at least not here. "Look around. This place is filled with guys a lot better looking and more interesting than me. Eric is amazing, and he wins competitions and stuff."

"He's also straight," Beckett growled with impatience.

"I get that, but most of the guys here are like him. They've done things and been places I've only dreamed of."

Val was still talking to the blond, paying little attention to me—maybe by accident, but more likely by design. I squeaked when Beckett's expression darkened and he grabbed my hand and pulled me through the gym toward the locker rooms. "What are you doing?"

"I'm going to show you something," Beckett said with determination. When we reached the locker room door, he pushed it open, banging it on the wall. The men inside all turned and Beckett met their gazes. "Get out now."

I had never in my life seen big guys look so scared. Hell, I was about to piss myself. I had no idea how Beckett would react when he was angry, and I wasn't sure I liked it. The men, however, raced to get out. Those dressed filed out past us, and the undressed raced to the shower and sauna area. "Do you do that often?"

"Sometimes there are benefits to being really big," Beckett said as he marched me up in front of the mirrors that lined a short wall near the locker room door. He positioned me so I faced it and stood behind me. "What do you see?"

"You," I answered quietly, nervous and wondering what he was up to.

"No. What do you see in yourself?" Beckett grabbed the tail of my T-shirt and yanked it over my head. For a second I crossed my arms over my chest, but Beckett gently held my arms and lowered them to my side. "What do you see?"

"I don't know. Me."

"Take a good look. I took an acting class once, and they had us do this. If we want to be able to play other people, we have to know

129

ourselves… or something like that. Personally, I think it was a chance for the old queen to get his jollies, but that's another story." I smiled and turned to Beckett, who gently turned my head back to the mirror. "What do you see?" he asked again. "Be honest."

"Just a guy," I answered with a shrug.

Beckett backed away and pulled off his shirt, standing next to me. "What do you see in me?"

I swallowed. "A gorgeous, talented, sexy man who I want to touch and taste until I can't see straight. I see someone who has his entire amazing life ahead of him, with limitless possibilities and a talent that can take him anywhere." Fuck, I wanted to turn and ask Beckett to take me right here, right now. But I forced myself to stay where I was, even though I watched every twitch of every muscle. "I see someone I can't take my eyes off of even when I'm across the room from you or sitting in the very back of a theater."

"Do you know what I see?" Beckett asked. I shook my head. "I see a guy who everyone thinks is huge and dumb. I always thought that was what I was. I was an athlete, so that meant I was bad in school, and I went with that. I see someone who always thought athletics was the only thing he was good at, and someone who had to hide who he really was."

"You're none of that. You're smart and talented and so very sexy. I wonder what you could possibly see in me." I turned to look at him, and Beckett gently placed his hands on my shoulders, turning me back around.

"What I see in you and what you see in me is less important than what we see in ourselves. I can't change what's in the mirror. Only you can do that. Just like only I can change what I see."

"I don't understand," I whispered. Guys began coming back inside, poking their heads around the corner and then backing out again.

"When you see yourself in the mirror, what's there?"

I looked deep and nodded. "Gaydie Paydie. He's what's there. I'm not overweight anymore, but he's still there, standing behind me. The kid I was."

"But he isn't there. You stand on your own two feet most of the time. You know what I see? A smaller man who's cute and caring, who raced out of bed to help a friend. You throw yourself into what you do, and you give everything you have to your work and what you think is important." He put his arms around me, and I leaned back into his warmth. "But you have to decide what you see in the mirror and what's important to you." Beckett leaned closer, and I felt his warm lips on my shoulder.

Beckett slipped away and he pulled on his shirt. Without another word, he left the locker room, the door closing behind him. I stood still, staring into the mirror as men came back around me.

"Where did you go?" Val asked as he skidded to a stop on the tile floor, nearly knocking me over. "Everyone is talking about Beckett dragging you in here, and they were taking bets on whether he was fucking you in here. Was he?"

I rolled my eyes. "No," I whispered. "I think I'm going to take a shower and walk home." I turned away from the mirror, knowing I was the center of everyone's attention, for a few minutes, anyway, and went to my locker. I opened it and got undressed before heading to the showers. Guys chattered and gossiped about what had been going on, but they quieted when I came close, which told me all I needed to know. I paid no attention. I just got into one of the shower stalls and cleaned up quickly. I could still feel where Beckett had touched me, my skin holding on to the last of his lingering warmth. By the time I was done, it was gone. I dried off and returned to my locker. My momentary notoriety having faded, no one paid me any mind as they went about their business, and I dressed, packed up my bag, and left the locker room.

I saw Val talking to the blond, who seemed really into him. I approached and told Val I was going.

"Lars says he'll make sure I get home."

"Okay, but call me when you leave." I wanted to make sure Val would be all right. He promised he would, and I left the gym, walking the darkened streets of the Village toward home. I needed to think. Well, more accurately, I needed to determine what I was going to do to show Beckett that I was starting to understand what he meant and that I wanted him back. But words weren't going to be enough.

FRIDAY I avoided everyone in the office, especially Garren. The phone was my best friend, and I beat the bushes to arrange auditions and ensure that my clients knew where to be and when.

Gloria walked into my office near the end of the day. "I think you and I need to talk," she said.

I motioned her to a chair, and she sat down rather carefully. "You have a gift for this business, young man. You can spot talent that others miss. I heard you signed those drag performers and were not only able to renegotiate their current contracts, but you got Vince Bradford to agree to see them. How did you do that?"

"I heard he was looking for some new show ideas, and I arranged for two tickets to be delivered to his home. It's well known that he also likes nubile young men, so Penny convinced Eye Candy from the cabaret to make the delivery, promising him a show he wouldn't soon forget." I smiled.

"Well, kid, it's brilliant, and if they're as good as you say…."

"Is that why you wanted to see me?"

"Keep your drawers on," she teased, settling back in the chair. "God, these are awful—like unwelcome guest chairs. I'll tell Claude to have Millie get something better for in here."

"Thanks, but…." I didn't want to be a bother.

"There are things you need to know," she began, leaning forward seriously. "Garren is after you. Don't know why, but he's spreading a rumor that you're dating a client. Are you?"

Just when I thought I'd seen light at the end of the tunnel and figured out what I wanted to do with Beckett, this came up again. "I was. Beckett is someone I knew from high school, and we met again at the gym and then when he came in here."

"Were you involved before you signed him?" Gloria asked.

"Of course not. I signed him because he's amazingly talented. Which he proved by landing a great role." Gloria nodded but said nothing. "I really like him, Gloria. He's smart, and he makes me scream and laugh, sometimes both at once."

"Son of a bitch," she swore.

"I know it's against the rules, and that's why I broke it off with him, but I'm miserable." I stood behind my desk. "I'm going to get him back. And I don't really care what Claude says. I won't give him up as a client because no one, not even you, could do a better job for him."

"What if he doesn't take you back?"

"I'm still the best for his career." I met her steely gaze. I was done with this crap. I knew what I wanted, and I wasn't going to let anyone stop me. "Garren is a weaselly piece of crap, a mediocre agent, and he spends more time worrying others are going to make him look bad than actually doing his job well."

"You just figured that out?" Gloria asked. I sat back down, a little stunned. "Of course I knew that. I see what people do in this office, the same as Claude does. He knows who's hustling and who's coasting and just getting by."

I nodded. "So what do I do?"

"I can't tell you that, just like I can't say how Claude will react. But, young man, I can tell you one thing: I've been doing this a long time, and I've met a great number of people. Believe it or not, I've spent a few nights with a client or two over the years."

"Did you regret it?" I asked.

She shook her head. "And thank you for not acting surprised. I was a real looker when I was young. This business and too many cigarettes aged me something awful. Well that, and that bitch called time. But no, I don't regret it. I was never in love with any of them, and they all thought getting me into bed would get them better parts. That was a laugh." She cackled like a hen, something I'd never heard or expected from her. "They were awful in bed and more interested in themselves than me. Never passed a mirror they didn't like."

I laughed with her. I could easily see that.

"No, I fell in love with a producer. I was working at a different agency, of course, and the boss, an awful, shriveled prune named Hilliard, didn't dare fire me because otherwise Monty would have ruined him. So we dated, but agreed never to use our influence to help each other. He gave my clients a fair shake, and I only sent him talent I thought he could use, just like anyone else. Ours was a relationship that existed outside the theater." Gloria fanned herself. "That man was a god, and I loved him to pieces."

"I'm not sure what you're trying to tell me, but you have some great stories."

She leaned even closer. "Don't let love get away from you for anything. Certainly not Claude, who's on wife number three and doesn't know squat about women. He's all about his job. His wives find out eventually, and they also realize the prenup they signed doesn't give them a thing." She laughed once again. "I had Monty for over thirty years, and I wouldn't change a thing. He was the love of my life, and you deserve that too.

"But you better know that relationships can go south, and you better have a clear understanding with this young man about what will happen should things not come up roses."

I smiled as excitement filled me. "I will."

"There's one more thing. You need to be honest with Claude and tell him. Secrets have a way of getting out at the worst time. If he knows and gives his blessing, you're covered and Garren becomes the blowhard he is." She covered her mouth with her hand as she coughed a few times.

"That's what I'm afraid of. What if he fires me?"

Gloria laughed and coughed once again. "You're bringing in new talent and have great instincts. That doesn't grow on trees. Just talk to him. He isn't going to bite your head off."

"Should I do it now?"

"Heavens, no. Make sure you get this dream man of yours back first. Why ask for something you may not need?"

I shook my head. "You sure know how to pop someone's bubble of hope."

Gloria stood with a mock evil grin. "That, young man, is part of what makes my life fun." She reached to open the door. "Yeah, I know I'm a bitch."

"That's just the image you project."

She stopped and turned at me, as serious as a heart attack. "That may be true, but if you tell anyone, so help me, I'll rip your balls off."

"Got it," I told her. She left, closing the door with more force than was necessary. For the remainder of the day, which was just a couple of hours, I received looks of sympathy from everyone in the office. I did nothing to alter their perception. The only one who acted different from the rest was Garren, who kept a cocky grin on his face that I wanted to punch away.

Val phoned as I left the office. "I should be home soon. I was wondering if you wanted to get dinner?" he asked.

"What about the blond from the gym?" I teased.

"He was nice and even asked me out. I gave him my number and said we could go out to the movies or something, but I want to double date or something, just to be safe." I could hear the worry in his voice. "What are you going to do this evening?"

"I don't know," I said as I got into the elevator. "What's the weather like?"

"Really nice. Sunny. I have the windows open to air the place out. Why?"

"I'll call you as I get closer." I hung up and shoved my phone into my pocket.

After leaving the building, I made my way to the subway, but it was jammed tight, so I turned around and started walking. I was lucky and caught a lot of the lights. I was surrounded by people for blocks, a crowd going in my general direction, but I was alone and had time to think. *Why am I being so hardheaded and such a chickenshit?* What really bothered me was my reluctance to take a chance. I had moved to New York on my own, away from my dad, in order to make my own life. That decision should have been a hell of a lot more scary than admitting I had feelings for Beckett.

"Gaydie Paydie is gone," I murmured under my breath.

"Hey, buddy, watch where you're going," a man in a designer suit called as I bumped into him at a corner, lost in my own thoughts.

"Sorry," I said, stepping slightly back as the guy smoothed his coat with his hand before signaling and then hurrying to where a taxi pulled to the curb. I stopped watching and continued on. I had a number of blocks to walk yet, and as the people thinned out, I could keep to my own pace and enjoy the city around me.

It was getting well toward dinnertime when I reached the edge of the Village. On the corner, a flower shop was about ready to close. I hurried inside and looked around.

"Can I help you?" a woman asked in that hurried tone that meant, "I want to go home."

"I need a bunch of flowers," I said and picked some colorful mixed blooms.

"What are you trying to say?"

"That I was a stupid idiot and that I'm starting to understand. I think."

The woman's gaze softened, and instantly she looked younger. When her lips pulled up, she seemed prettier. "Are these for a lady?"

"My boyfriend," I told her. "Well, at least I hope he'll be my boyfriend. I broke up with him because I was scared and used my job as an excuse. I used to be fat, and he's drop-dead gorgeous, and I thought he would get tired of me, and, well…." I gasped for air, and she had the decency to chuckle.

"It's all right. I used to be on the heavy side myself."

I widened my gaze, because there was no sign of that now.

"Thanks for that."

"What?"

"That look. It's nice to see, and for the record—" She stepped back and gave me the same look. "—you're as cute as they come, so forget all that 'I used to be fat' stuff. Now, as for flowers… roses always work. I have deep lavender. They're rich-looking and not the usual."

"Perfect." I paid while she wrapped them up. "Thank you so much," I told her with a wave as I left the shop. On the sidewalk, I fumbled in my bag and located Beckett's address before making my way to his place. I knew he was staying with friends and I hoped he was home and that they wouldn't mind me stopping by.

I reached the building and found the apartment, rang the bell and then stepped back. A woman pushed the door open and peered out half a minute later.

"I'm sorry to bother you. I was looking for Beckett," I told her in as friendly a tone as I could muster over every nerve firing all at once. "I'm Payton, by the way."

She nodded. "I'm sorry. He got home from the theater half an hour ago and then left again with a guy from the gym. He said he was going out for the evening. Did you try calling him?"

"I wanted to surprise him, but… I'm sorry to bother you. Thanks so much." I turned and walked back to toward the corner. I should have called instead of using most of what remained of my grocery money on flowers and rushing right over.

I held my flowers and bag as I walked through the twilight-colored streets to home. I managed to pull out my phone and call Val.

"Maybe we should get takeout or something for dinner. I wonder how roses would taste."

"What does that mean?" Val asked. I approached the building and saw Val standing out front with his phone to his ear. He put it away when he saw me, and I shrugged and held up the package of flowers. "Where were you?"

"At Beckett's."

"Why?" Val asked.

"I made up my mind about what I wanted, but he wasn't home." I waited while Val held the door open. "I'm going to put these in water and then get some dinner. At least I don't have tickets for the theater tonight, just two performances tomorrow, and one on Sunday. I want a drink, food, and then to crawl into a hole where I won't make a fool of myself in front of a stranger."

"So he wasn't home. That's no big deal," Val said as I unlocked my door.

"His roommate said he came home from rehearsal and was out with a guy from the gym."

"It could have been the guy he was with yesterday. He was so straight it wasn't even funny." Val plopped down on the sofa and looked at me expectantly.

I opened the refrigerator and pulled out two beers, then handed him one. "I'm just a fool."

"You're overreacting," Val said as he settled back on the sofa while I got down the one vase I had. It was plain glass from a small arrangement I'd gotten for my birthday a few months ago. I had intended to use it on the patio once I set it up. I filled it with water, cut the ends of the stems, and placed them in the vase.

"I'll order Chinese," Val said. "It'll take a few minutes, but Golden Crown delivers pretty quickly. Or we could order and walk to pick it up."

"I've walked enough for one day." I sat next to Val and opened my beer.

"Okay. I'll go get it. You call."

"The usual?"

"Yeah, broccoli beef and General Tso," Val said, and I nodded, pulled out my phone, and placed the order.

"I know I have no right to be upset," I admitted to Val once I'd hung up. "It wasn't like I'd told him I loved him or that we'd made promises to each other, but... I...."

"You know, it doesn't matter what you've said to each other. It's what you feel that counts. The words are communication and validation, but they don't mean that what you feel is any less real."

"The proverbs of Val," I quipped. Granted, it wasn't very good.

"Before I forget, they said they have another delivery nearby, so you don't need to go get the food."

"Good." Val emptied his bottle and waved it in the air. I took the hint and got him another. I only had two left, but that would do through dinner, and neither of us needed to get anything beyond a little tipsy.

"Are you really okay after last weekend? You can talk about it if you want." He'd been quiet about the whole thing with Rod.

"It sucks, but you and Beckett arrived in time, and even my wrists have almost healed." He sighed and put the bottle on the table. "If you want the truth, I haven't been able to sleep in my own bed since it happened. I've stayed on the sofa, and my back is killing me, but I can't bear the thought of sleeping in that bed again. I know he's gone, and I feel so dumb, but I can barely go into my bedroom. I tried. Last night I went to bed and lay there, wondering if someone was going to come into the room." Val began to shake, and I set my bottle aside and hugged him.

"He's gone and no one is going to get in and hurt you. Have you thought about talking to someone?"

"You mean a shrink? No. I keep hoping things will fade. If it had happened someplace else, I could stay away, but it was my home and my bedroom." Val leaned against me. "I need to man up and just stay in bed. Since I don't have to work, I was going to try this weekend. Eventually I'll get tired enough to fall asleep."

"Sweetheart...."

"It's the only way. I simply have to force myself to get over it all." Val stayed where he was for a few minutes, then reached for his bottle. "It would be so easy to drink myself to sleep." I inhaled loudly, and Val chuckled. "I won't, I promise. Besides, I don't want to endure all those noogies."

"You know I'll do whatever I can to help." I wished there was something I could do to make all this go away, but Val had to do it on his own. The memories of what had happened were too fresh, but they would fade in time. "You need to give it some time."

"Bullshit," Val said, jumping to his feet. "I can't sleep in my own bed." He was yelling and shaking at the same time. "He took that from me, and all you have to say is to give it time. I want to feel normal and happy again." He relaxed a little. "I was talking to that really super cute guy at the gym. He was way hot, but I just kept wondering if he was going to hurt me. When he asked for my number, I almost ran for the locker room."

"But you didn't," I said, just above a whisper.

"No. I didn't."

"And next time it will get easier. That's how these things work. Little steps."

Val smiled a little. "You could give yourself that same advice."

"I know. I kept waiting for the grand illumination."

"Wait, the what?" Val asked, looking at me like I'd lost my mind.

"You know, like in the movies, when everything falls into place. You can see it in their melodramatic eyes. They turn around, rush back to wherever they'd been, and confess that they'd been stupid all along and should have seen the love that was right in front of their face. It happens in every chick flick ever made."

"And you tear up each time," Val said.

"Yeah, I know, but that's not the point. See, I kept waiting for that moment. I thought everything would fall into place and I would be able to have it all—a great job, a nice apartment, and the hottest guy I've ever met. The trifecta."

"How about the best friend ever? Where does that fit in?" Val asked dubiously.

"Okay the four-fecta. God, that sounds dirty."

"Get your four-fecta in here," Val said in a deep voice before cackling like a loon.

"I didn't think it was that funny."

"It wasn't. I'm humoring you," Val said.

I whapped him with one of the old couch pillows, grateful a cloud of dust didn't fill the room. I really needed to clean. "Anyway," I said exaggeratedly. "The point, before we got way off into the weeds, is that I was waiting for the lightbulb moment, and there wasn't one."

"Oh."

"It's good. See, I think I get it now. The light doesn't come in a moment. Sometimes the light has to weave and work its way over and under all the walls and car wrecks that we hold on to in order to protect ourselves, and that takes time. If we're lucky, it manages to complete the obstacle course through our emotional crap, and then we understand that we've been idiots."

"And that happened to you? The light made it?"

"Yeah, hence the flowers, but it could be too late," I said.

"If it is, then the next time the light won't take so long. Or you won't need it because you'll be ready for the good stuff," Val said.

"I hope so, and I hope you are too." I took his hands. "Don't let Rod stop you from being who you are. He was a jerk with issues of his own, and he has to deal with them. You need to let yourself be happy and not let him add another piece of baggage to the emotional crap pile."

"I don't have one," Val said, and I snorted. "Okay. I have a little one."

"Everest little," I quipped.

Val tilted his head slightly, but he didn't argue. "Okay. I promise I'll sleep in my own room tonight and not let Rod spoil what could be a chance with Lars."

I snickered. I couldn't help it.

"What? He's Scandinavian, and you saw the way he looked in that T-shirt." Val pulled his hands away from mine. "And the way he filled out those shorts...."

"Okay. Val is officially back."

"Yes. But I'm still not going out with him alone. Not the first time. I'm going to be smart and take my time. I will not sleep with a guy on the first date... anymore." Val raised his hand as if he were a Boy Scout, except, as I remember, none of their oaths involved sluttiness. *A Scout is trustworthy, loyal, helpful, friendly, courteous, kind, obedient, cheerful, thrifty, brave, clean, reverent... and not a slut.* Maybe the last part was implied.

A knock on the door interrupted us. Val jumped up and raced for the door. Someone from the building must have been leaving and let them in. "I'll get it," he said as he reached into his pockets for some cash. He left the door open, and I heard him paying and thanking the delivery guy before coming back inside.

"You were hoping it was Beckett, weren't you? Don't deny it—I saw that flash of hope."

"Okay, I did for a second," I admitted, glancing at the flowers.

"I'm sure everything is going to be fine." Val set the bag on the coffee table, and I got plates from the kitchen and brought the last two beers in the fridge. Val dished out the food and then turned on the television. We watched reruns of *Chopped* while we ate.

Once he was done, Val went up to his place and returned with a pitcher of some pink concoction that we proceeded to work our way through. I cut Val off before we could get too drunk and made sure he made it up the stairs, then locked all the doors and went to bed myself.

I should have known the drinking would be too much. I was hearing things. A gentle tinking on the small window that faced the street. I had a love/hate relationship with that window. It let in a little light when the curtains were open, which I liked, but it also meant everyone on the street could see into my place. I needed to get some blinds for it, but hadn't yet.

The tinking sound came again, and I cracked my eyes open, listening. God, I hoped it wasn't some homeless guy looking for a handout. I got out of bed and carefully walked across the room, peering out through the side of the curtain. I didn't see anyone. The rapping sounded once more, and I jumped back, ending up sprawled on the sofa cushion. I pulled the curtain aside, grateful for the decorative iron work on the window, and peered out.

"What are you doing here?" I asked as Beckett stared back at me.

"They said you stopped by, and…." I heard faintly through the glass. I motioned toward the door and buzzed Beckett into the building, then unlocked the door. I didn't have a chance to open it. Beckett came through like a freight train. "Shawna said that you had knocked just after I left and that you had flowers with you," Beckett whispered into my neck. He already had me in his arms and lifted off my feet. I wrapped my legs around his waist, and Beckett put a hand on my butt to steady me. I looked toward the table.

"I did. They were for you, but you were gone."

"I'm right here."

"There isn't anyone else?" I asked, needing the reassurance.

"There hasn't been in a while, and there wasn't going to be. When I first kissed you, you set me on fire. I couldn't be with anyone else until I knew you were gone for good."

"But...."

Beckett knocked the door closed and carried me to the bed, laying me down, but I kept my legs where they were. I wouldn't let go.

"I saw how you looked at me at the gym, how you've always looked at me," Beckett said.

"Everyone looks at you, and they will even more once your play opens. How can anyone not look at you?"

Beckett chuckled. "You think everyone sees the same things you do." He kissed me hard. I squirmed. "What?" Beckett growled. "This is kissing time, not talking time," He kissed me harder. I might have tasted blood, but I certainly tasted Beckett, manly musk mixed with a hint of beer, tinged with soap, cologne, and God knew what else. I clung to him, wanting more.

"Are you gonna fuck me now?"

Beckett backed away. "I'm going to make love to you now," he corrected, and goddamn if the light didn't go on, bright as all hell.

CHAPTER 8—LOVE

HE'D BEEN the one to say the *L* word first. I didn't know why that was important, but it was. He'd actually said it.

"What are you grinning at?" Beckett said, pulling back from the kiss, but still holding me in his amazingly strong arms.

"You said you loved me. What's better to grin about?" I answered, and then realized I was waiting for him to clarify what he'd said or to say I misheard him.

"I guess it is," he said, grinning back at me.

"Is that it?" I asked.

"If you expected fireworks, I'll be getting to those in a little while once you decide the time for talking is over and the time for me to make you moan my name while I'm buried deep inside you has begun."

"I like that time."

"Me too." His lips hovered right above mine, and he opened his mouth, teasing my lips with the very tip of his tongue. I opened my mouth and sucked on his tongue, taking him in.

Beckett pulled back just enough to whisper, "Are you done talking for now?"

"I guess." I wrapped my arms around his neck and pulled him down. Talking was overrated. I kissed him almost as hard as he'd kissed me, tugging on his lower lip.

"You guess?" Beckett asked, teasing me. "You need to stop worrying so much."

"I know."

"And maybe stop thinking so much. You chew on everything until all the flavor's gone and then wonder what happened. Just enjoy and be happy with what you're given, because sometimes you win the jackpot if you're willing to see it."

That was one sentiment I could agree with. I seemed to have won a giant jackpot, and as that winner, I got to lose my pants. I smiled as that thought flicked through my head. Beckett slid his hand into my sleep pants, shoving them down over my butt. He left them there, spreading my cheeks, tapping my opening lightly as I whined softly.

I let go of Beckett and grabbed at his shirt, tugging it upward. He released me, and I managed to get his shirt over his head before working on his pants. My hands shook as I got the damn things opened and shoved them down his legs, Beckett's cock springing out. I went for it, sucking him as deep as I could.

"God, your lips are pure magic."

I hummed some sort of agreement, tasting all of him.

Beckett pushed me back, and my lips slipped from around him.

"What was that for?" I asked as he did some kind of dance to get out of his pants. Then he placed his hand on the center of my chest and climbed on the bed, straddling me, guiding his cock to my greedy lips. Fuck and hell. That was one amazing sight. Beckett, all muscle and ripples, as he slipped his cock between my lips. All that power hovered above me, and it was mine—he was all mine.

I got comfortable and sucked him in, cupping his weighty balls. One thing I really loved about Beckett was the way he kept everything manscaped. His balls were smooth, and I caressed them with my fingers. "Put your hands behind your head for me," I said after taking a deep breath. "Oh, yeah, that's gorgeous." Beckett thrust his chest out, and I took him in deep. He moved his hips slowly, rolling his belly, his abs becoming more pronounced as he moved.

Beckett lowered his arms. I growled at the loss of my view, but then it turned to a whimper when Beckett reached behind himself, sliding his hand down my belly, moving my loose sleep pants aside and grabbing my cock firmly in his hand. He stroked me while I sucked on his balls, the silky orbs popping in and out of my mouth. Beckett slowly withdrew, leaning down to kiss me while positioning me so my head was on the pillow. Then he sat back, staring at me. At moments like these, I was never sure if I should be embarrassed or not. Too often I slipped into the image of myself as I used to be.

"Don't," Beckett murmured, taking my hands gently in his. "I know what you're thinking."

"It's hard not to," I whispered.

"I know. Our vision of ourselves is always difficult to change, but you did the hard part already. The package has changed already. You need to see yourself the way the rest of us see you."

"I know."

Beckett leaned closer, and I shivered with heat and excitement. "You don't. It isn't what you look like, because I'd like you no matter what. It's the person you are. That's what matters, and you can be so fierce. I like that."

"So you're saying…."

"Just let yourself be you and be happy. Accept that I'm not going anywhere unless you tell me to go. I don't have one eye on you and the other on the door." I had said something like that, I remembered, and I wondered for a second if Beckett had heard me. "I know how people are here. But that's not me." He leaned closer, pressing against my bare chest.

"It's hard to accept sometimes, but I'm trying. Maybe if you showed me."

"Baby, I'll show you again and again, for as long as you'll let me," Beckett told me. He shucked my sleep pants down my legs, and I got them off. They crumpled to the floor, but I paid little attention. Beckett rolled us on the bed so I was lying on top of his mountain of muscle. "I want to taste you."

"Yeah," I said, my voice quivering along with the rest of me. I knelt around him and Beckett cradled my ass, bringing me closer. I thought he meant sucking my cock, but he guided my ass to his mouth and drove deep. I screamed with pleasure I couldn't hold inside any longer. I clamped my hand over my mouth, biting it to keep from waking the entire building. "Jesus," I whimpered, resting my hands on Beckett's thick legs to keep from tumbling backward. Breathing was difficult, and got more so when Beckett gripped my cock, stroking me as he rimmed me to the point where seeing straight was difficult. "I had no idea...."

"You will, baby," Beckett crooned, blowing hot breath on my wet skin. "Show me you like it."

"Yeah."

He slipped what I guessed was his pinkie into me. I gasped, wide-mouthed, not knowing what the hell to concentrate on. His hand, the finger, his lips—all of it threatened to overwhelm me. "Come for me, baby. You're strung too tight. I want you nice and relaxed when I fill you, because I intend to stay inside this tightness." He withdrew his finger and inserted a thicker one.

I threw my head back and moaned loudly, trying to control the rising tide. I couldn't. Gasping, I thrust my hips, pressing my cock into his hand for that little bit of extra sensation... I went flying within seconds. I remembered coming, my brain sizzling as excitement and heat bloomed throughout me. I remembered Beckett being there, holding me, and then the floaty feeling as afterglow settled in. I was afraid to move in case this wonderfulness ended, but it didn't.

Gently, Beckett moved me until I lay on the bedding. He stroked my belly and chest as I kept my eyes closed, luxuriating in the warmth and intimacy of a simple touch.

Slowly the warmth and buzz began to fade. Beckett was right there. He took me into his arms, shared a smile, and then kissed me, hard. I could feel his excitement, his cock sliding along my hip. But even more pronounced was the energy that raced through him. "Beck...."

"You do this to me," Beckett whispered. "I'm likely to fly apart at any second, and that's all because of you."

"Me?"

"Oh, yes. You do this to me. Make no mistake about it. I can't get enough of you. At night when I'm home, I think of you."

"I dreamed of you... a lot." I slipped my arms behind his neck and then down his back, muscles rippling beneath my touch.

"Can you feel that? Even when I can't see you, my body knows your touch. It aches for it." He crushed me closer, holding me, petting me. I wrapped my legs around his waist, opening myself to him. I felt rather than saw Beckett reach for the drawer next to the bed. I closed my eyes. I didn't want anything to intrude on the fantasy of being with Beckett at that very moment. I heard the package open and felt his slight fumble as he prepared himself, and then his breath was back, warm against my lips. I held still with anticipation, waiting. Beckett pressed against me and then slowly entered, stretching me.

The burn was magnificent, something I had begun to fear I would never feel again. Beckett was a big man, and I adored the way he filled me. "Yes," I whispered.

"I won't hurt you."

"Never hurt," I whispered back, holding Beckett's shoulders, digging my fingers into the flesh as he sank deeper and deeper inside me. I kissed him. It was sloppy, and in the middle, I cried out. Beckett stilled and then continued. I rolled my head back and forth on the pillow, holding Beckett and breathing through my mouth until his hips pressed to my butt. "God," I breathed. "You're huge."

"Too big?"

"No such thing. I like you big," I whispered and held Beckett firmly. He made love to me slowly, deeply. There was no rush. At times I wanted to scream at him to go faster, to move more, but he had his own internal pace, and no pleading would make him go faster. When I did beg, he simply kissed away my words and continued at his infuriatingly measured pace, pushing me to the edge, but never over.

"Not yet," Beckett scolded, brushing my hand away from my cock yet again.

"I need it," I whined.

"So do I," Beckett confessed.

"Then why aren't you going faster? Fuck me, for God's sake!"

"Pushy bottom," Beckett said, snapping his hips hard, and I grunted and sighed at the same time.

"Damn controlling top," I countered. "I think I read somewhere that the guy on the bottom was really the one in control, so get on with it." I gritted my teeth and clenched hard around Beckett. He gasped and I held him tight. "That's more like it." Beckett sprawled over me, holding my hands in one of his, lips right above me, snapping his hips, sending ripples of desire through me as his cock slid across the spot inside.

My head felt ready to explode. I tried to wrench my hands away, but he held them just tightly enough that I couldn't get free easily. Not that I really wanted to. Beckett's eyes glassed over, his body glistening with sweat. He smelled amazing, powerful. I breathed through my nose to take in all of him.

"Oh God!"

"You got that right," I whispered hoarsely. "Now let me go so I can come when you do."

Beckett released my hands, and I began stroking myself. Beckett's movements were ragged, and I could tell he was seconds away. It wasn't long and I was right there with him, the tingling starting at the base of my spine, radiating outward.

"Come on, baby, let me see you go," Beckett said.

I squeezed lightly, twisting my hand around the head of my cock, and tumbled right over the edge. I felt Beckett come with me. My body tightened and spasmed, my release painting my chest and belly. When it passed and the warm glow took over, I clutched Beckett to me and held him as tight as I dared.

"Am I crushing you?" Beckett whispered.

"Maybe a little," I admitted, and he rolled us on the bed so I could use him like a hard mattress. I didn't move an inch, listening to him breathe, letting our musky sex scent wrap comfortingly around us.

After a few minutes, Beckett shifted and took care of the condom, dropping it in the bin near the bed. "We better clean up," Beckett said, but my eyes had drifted half closed. I didn't want to move. Beckett had other ideas, and he sat up, taking me with him. "I can carry you."

"Don't you dare! I'm not a doll and you're not a Neanderthal."

"Then come on," Beckett said, standing and tugging me up into his arms. "Let's get wet. I'll make sure you are good and clean."

Wet with Beckett—now *that* I was up for. I led him into my small bathroom. The tub was standard sized and I wondered exactly how I was going to find room with Beckett in it. He started the water and stepped under the spray. When I followed him in, he hugged me tightly to him, and I had my answer.

I got some soap, rubbing it between my hands, lathering up well before stroking over Beckett's strong chest. "I love this, you know."

"What?"

"That you're big, strong, and yet gentle with me." Hell, I loved that his muscles danced under my hands. Some big guys were too much, their chests way too developed. "You know, you look more like a Marine than anything else. A big Marine. A guy who earned his muscles."

"I've done plenty of hard work in my life. I didn't get my body just in the gym. I had to use gyms to get ready for competition, but that was mostly BS stuff. It's politics, and whether this muscle and that muscle look just right. Most of those guys juice, and that wasn't what I wanted."

I continued downward, washing his belly, which was nearly as hard as his chest. I knew mine was soft, if relatively flat, but not his. "Turn around," I whispered. "And put your hands on the wall for me."

"What do you have in mind?" Beckett asked as he turned. I soaped my hands once again and started down his wide back, soaping his smooth skin, loving the flex of his muscles, knowing he cared about me and that all this power could be unleashed, but that I had nothing at all to worry about.

Beckett's ass. What could I say? Bubbles would be jealous. I soaped it two or three times, copping a feel, kneading the cheeks, pressing to his back so my reawakening cock rested along his cleft. I slid my still soapy hands around to his stomach and left them there. "I love you, Beck," I whispered. "Please don't turn around," I said when I felt him move. "You always hold me, and that comes with being so much bigger, but now I get to hold you and I like it." Beckett put his hands over mine, and I closed my eyes. Beckett slowly stepped backward, and I did the same, the water sluicing over both of us, washing away the soap. My erection abated, which was fine. I didn't have the energy to go again. What I wanted was right here.

"Baby," Beckett whispered, and this time he did turn around. He lathered his hands, and then it was my turn to receive a very thorough washing. When Beckett knelt to get my legs, his magic fingers revived my dick, and once it was pointing upward, he leaned in and slid his lips along my shaft.

"Beck, I don't…." God, I wondered if I had it in me, but the sight of Beckett on his knees was too much to resist. He sucked me and washed up my legs to my butt, massaging the cheeks as he took me deeper. Breathless, I stood still and let him take me for an amazing ride. When I came, I would have fallen if Beckett hadn't caught me, held me up, and rinsed me off before turning off the water.

Beckett reached for towels, and I grinned. My bath towels looked like hand towels on him. My legs decided to cooperate, so I patted his back dry, and then he did the same for me. I opened the bathroom door and was assaulted by the sex smell from the rest of the apartment.

"Jesus," Beckett whispered.

"Give me a minute." I opened the small closet next to the bathroom door and pulled out a fresh set of sheets. I stripped the bed and put the old sheets in the laundry hamper in the corner of the bathroom. Then I remade the bed with Beckett watching me the entire time. I tried not to feel self-conscious, especially when the towel I'd been wearing slipped to the floor. Beckett picked up the towel and hung it in the bathroom. By the time he returned, I had the bed made and was changing pillowcases. He'd opened the door to the patio a little way, and fresh air drifted in.

"I love the way you smell," Beckett said after closing and locking the door once again. His massive arms enveloped me. "And I love holding you."

"We need to go to bed. Do you have rehearsal tomorrow?"

"They asked me to be there at ten for some one-on-one time with the director," Beckett said, and I snuggled closer into his warmth. "Kendall is flying to LA for some work this weekend, so we're going to run some blocking. Hiram seems very pleased and asked if I could spare a few hours tomorrow for some fine-tuning. Is that typical?"

"Each director has their own style."

"Hiram said he has another show that will go into production after this one, and there's a part that could be perfect for me. I really like him. He's loud sometimes, but he's good and he gives direction really well. There's no ulterior motive or trying to find out what he really wants. I like that." Beckett released me and got into bed. I climbed in after him, and instantly Beckett was there with me, an arm around my waist, hand on my belly. He yawned. "Do you want to do something after I'm done?"

"I have theater tickets for tomorrow afternoon and evening. You can come with me, if you like." I followed Beckett's lead, yawning as well. "The matinee is for one of the big Broadway shows. I forget which one, but that should be fun."

"No drag?" Beckett asked sleepily.

"Not that I expect," I told him, closing my eyes. Beckett kissed my shoulder, and I slowly rolled over. He kissed me again, gently, and I fell into a deep, contented sleep.

A KNOCK on the door startled me awake. "Payton."

"Just a second." My eyelids felt like sandpaper. I got up and pulled on my sleep pants, after finding them under the edge of the bed. I tied them and then opened the door. "Yeah, Val?"

"I was wondering if you wanted to go to breakfast." He peered inside and then at me. "Do you have company?" He looked at the room divider that created my bedroom.

"Yes." I checked the time. "Beckett came by after you left."

"So that was you I heard," Val said with a grin. "I was hoping so."

"God," I whispered. I checked the clock, groaning. It was way too early on a Saturday morning. "How about breakfast tomorrow?"

"Sure." Val smiled and then turned to leave.

"Why don't you set up your double date with your friend from the gym? Maybe for next weekend."

"With Beckett and you?" Val whispered, and I nodded. That lifted Val's spirits, and he bounded up the stairs. I closed the door and climbed back into bed. Beckett hugged me close and growled, pulling at the sleep pants until he had them off me. What a wake-up call.

Once Beckett left for the theater, I got some cleaning done in the apartment. It needed it. I also did laundry and the other mundane things in life, which in New York could be a chore. I ate a quick lunch, and when Beckett called to say that he wouldn't be done until one, I agreed to meet him at the theater and said we'd head to the show from there. I rode the subway downtown and emerged a block from where Beckett was working. He was waiting out front, and we fell into easy step together.

"How did you get the tickets for *Matilda*?"

"Another potential client. This one has a pretty major role and is looking for new representation. I'm not familiar with him, so he got me tickets." We stopped at Seventh Avenue. "Do you need some lunch?"

"I better get something," Beckett said. We stopped for a couple of kosher hot dogs, which Beckett tried not to inhale but did anyway. He must have been starved. I got him some water, and we continued to the theater. We waited outside for them to open the doors.

"Hi, guys." I turned to see if that was meant for us and groaned. Garren stood just a few feet away. "Taking your *client* to the theater again?"

Beckett shifted closer. I was glad he was there, but pissed that Garren was as well.

"Are you following me?" I asked.

"Please." Garren rolled his eyes. "I took Claude's advice to heart, and he passed on some extra tickets. I didn't know I was going to see you." I could already see the wheels turning in Garren's head.

"You okay?" Beckett whispered.

"Yeah. You remember Garren from my office."

Beckett held out his hand, and Garren shook it for about a second. The line began to move, and we headed into the theater. I bought a soda before we made our way to our seats. I was supremely glad Garren wasn't sitting anywhere near us.

"What's with that guy?"

"He's lazy, and he thinks he can get ahead by taking out anyone he sees as competition. A few weeks ago I wasn't on his radar, but now I am because of you and a few others."

"So?" Beckett asked, shifting in a seat that was definitely made for someone smaller than him.

"I'm breaking the rules by dating a client, and he thinks that he has some leverage against me now."

Beckett's expression became very serious. "Are we back there again?"

"No." I inhaled deeply. "I've decided to talk to Claude and tell him about you and me. I was hoping to give us a few weeks, but...." I figured it was best to be honest. "This is so new, and I didn't know you were going to come over last night.... Anyway, I wanted to make sure things were truly good between us before I talked to Claude. But I plan to tell him. It's less of a conflict if everyone knows and we're out in the open. But I wanted to talk to you about it first." I looked up at the stage. "I guess I was hoping we could do it in a better place than a theater."

"I think it's perfect. This is Garren's little melodrama, so why not have it happen here?" Beckett took my hand. "You talk to Claude and tell him whatever you need to. I'll be there too, if you want."

"You will?" I asked, more than a little surprised.

"Unless what you said last night was the sex talking," Beckett whispered into my ear, and damn if just the way he said "sex" wasn't enough to get me going. I shifted a little to try to get comfortable.

"It wasn't and you know it. I'm just nervous about how Claude will react." I knew what Gloria had said, but it still worried me. I wanted it all—my job, Beckett as a client, Beckett in my bed, in my life. Maybe I couldn't have it and would need to make a choice. Hell,

154

I'd already made the wrong one once before, when I let Beckett go. That wasn't an option this time. God, I hoped Gloria was right.

"Stop being nervous. That's just that Garren guy messing with your head." Beckett threaded his fingers into mine. "On Monday I'm not expected until ten. I'll go in with you, and we can talk to Claude together. That should put an end to Garren and all his petty mischief." Beckett gently touched my chin. "As long as that's what you want."

"I think I need to talk to Claude by myself, but thank you for offering to go with me, and yes, you're what I want," I whispered to him. "I'm just not used to getting everything I want. Usually something goes to hell." But at that moment I was extremely happy as I sat back to enjoy the show.

The actor I was there to see did an amazing job, and I made a note to get back to him first thing on Monday morning so I could find out what he needed me to do for him. I half watched for Garren as we left, and I was a little relieved that I didn't see him.

"What are you supposed to see tonight?" Beckett asked.

"Something I'm not hopeful about, but I got the tickets from Claude, so I have to go." I wanted to go back to my apartment and spend the evening in bed with Beckett. Instead, we got dinner and he accompanied me to a play that had me yawning halfway through. I did something I rarely do—left the theater at intermission. That train wreck wasn't going to get any more interesting, no matter what.

Sunday's performance was better, but unfortunately the person I'd been there to see had been shifted out of that performance, so I once again left at intermission and headed home. Beckett had left that morning because he had things to do, and I spent much of the day alone. Val came down for dinner, and we had a good time.

"So are you and Beckett together?" he asked from the sofa.

"He told me he loved me," I said.

Val squealed like a teenage girl, which of course had me doing the same thing. "So everything is good?"

"Yeah. I need to tell my boss about us tomorrow. Gloria said I shouldn't keep it a secret, and she's right. I'm just nervous. Beckett said he'd go with me if I needed him to, but this is my job and my decision, so I need to face the music."

"Do you think it will be that bad?" Val asked.

"I don't know, and I'm nervous about it." I had purposely not had anything stronger than soda, but now I was wired on caffeine. I finished my glass and went to get some water. "Gloria thinks it won't be that big a deal, though Garren obviously believes it's something he can use against me."

"You know, worrying won't help."

"I know, and I've been through every argument I can think of in my head half a million times." I sat back down and wished like hell Beckett was here with me.

"When is Beckett's opening night?" Val asked.

"Saturday night." That only added to my nerves. I was going to fly apart within seconds if I didn't calm down.

"Take it one thing at a time. You know you have to talk to your boss, so do it right away, and get it over with. At least then you'll know where you stand and you can deal with it."

I knew Val was right, but that didn't calm the butterflies in my belly. For the first time in my life I knew exactly what I wanted, I was happy, and I didn't want it to end.

I WOKE early Monday morning and went right into the office. I wanted to have my day organized and my plans set before my big talk with Claude.

"I need to see you in my office," Claude said sternly as I walked through the front door. He had to have been watching for me. Great.

"Let me drop my things," I told him and hurried to my office. I checked my schedule quickly and then raced back to Claude's office, closing the door behind me.

"What do you think you're doing?" he began, even before I could sit in one of the chairs. "Garren called me yesterday and told me that you're dating your clients and that he's seen you out more than once with them. We don't do that." Claude was red-faced and his head seemed about to explode. "I thought you were smarter than that and showed a lot of promise. But decisions like those are not conducive to the business of this office."

I lowered myself into one of the office chairs. "Excuse me?" I began. "Garren called you on a Sunday to tattle because he'd seen me at the theater with Beckett?"

"He said it was more than one client," Claude said forcefully.

"Well, Garren doesn't know crap," I fired back. "And he's a jealous little weasel who's mad because I turned him down."

"I beg your pardon?" That was apparently news to him.

"Yes. He asked me out, but I suggested we could go to the theater together as friends. He hated the play and made a scene in the lobby. Furthermore, doesn't it seem strange that he would call you on a Sunday because one of your employees was out on a date?" My heart pounded in my ears as I tried to keep all of this from exploding in my face.

"So you aren't dating your clients?"

"That's what I wanted to talk to you about. Beckett Huntington."

"Your new client."

"He and I went to high school together, and we've started seeing each other." I swore Claude looked ready to explode again, but I had to continue. "I planned to come in today and tell you about it."

"You were," Claude said flatly.

"Yes. I love my job and I'm good at it. But I love Beckett as well, and I'm not giving him up, either as a boyfriend or as his agent. He's aware of it, and now so are you. There's nothing secret or hidden about it. I have no idea where things will go with Beckett, but either way it won't affect my ability to do my job."

"Wait a minute," Claude said. I could see him calming down. "When you got that young man a job, were you already seeing him?"

"No. It happened afterward.

"What about this other man you were out with?"

"Claude, I didn't know my personal life was completely open to everyone in the office. I don't know what Garren saw, nor do I care. But I have to ask again, why is this so important to Garren that he feels he needs to call you about it on your day off?" I intended to keep the pressure on him for as long as possible. "Can I ask you something? When you decided to let Jane go, was there a similar type of incident with Garren, where he was feeding you information?" I don't know why I asked, but the expression on his face told me I'd hit a bull's-eye.

Claude cleared his throat. "Jane isn't the topic of discussion, and that was a different situation."

"But Garren did figure into it?"

He didn't answer, but he didn't have to. I had my answer.

"I intend to see Beckett. I walked away from him once because I was afraid of losing my job, based on something Garren said. I've brought in a lot of new talent, as you said last week, and I have more talent that's interested in coming our way."

"But dating clients is against the rules. You knew that."

"I didn't set out to date him. Heck, when I first met him, I loathed him. It's a long story, but it comes down to this: If you want to fire me, go ahead. I'll find another job and take my clients with me."

"There's no need to fly off the handle," Claude said as he leaned forward. "What concerns me is what happens if this relationship ends or if you have two clients up for a role. Which one will you push?"

"The director and producer make casting decisions, not me. Yes, I'll be dating Beckett, but if there's a conflict, I'll talk to you and we'll figure it out."

"This is a tough business, and people can be cruel. It's always best to avoid the appearance of impropriety."

"I understand. But if we're out in the open and it's general knowledge, then there's no issue." God, I hoped that was true. Claude put his hand to his brow. "Besides, I think you have a bigger issue than who I'm dating." I figured I might as well go for broke.

"How so?" Claude asked.

I didn't want to mention Gloria's name. It wasn't fair to her, and if Claude was really as blind to what was happening in his own office, then he probably wouldn't believe me if I told him. "I think a lot of this drama could have been avoided without the interference of a certain other person, and I think you know it too. Everyone in this office works hard and does an excellent job. It's why this is one of the top talent agencies in the city, and why it's still growing."

"True…." Claude sat back in his chair.

I took that as my cue to leave. I was pretty sure I'd kept my job, and he hadn't said anything more about seeing Beckett, so I decided I was ahead at the moment and was happy for things to stay that way. I left the office and was on my way to mine when Millie hurried up behind me and directed me to the lobby.

"Claude wants you again," she said, and I sighed. I should have known it was too good to be true. I stopped by the lobby and saw Beckett in the waiting area through the glass. I pushed open the door, surprised to see him.

"Why are you here?"

"Did you see him yet?" Beckett asked right away.

"Yes, and he wants to see me again."

"Then I'm going with you," Beckett answered firmly. "I'm a client of this firm, and he needs to hear what I have to say."

"You know he could let you out of your contract."

"Then he's a fool," Beckett said, louder than necessary.

"I am no fool, Mr. Huntington." Claude joined us, and I willed the floor to swallow me whole. Claude had a half smile cocked onto his lips. "Why don't both of you step into my office?"

I shared a glance at Beckett and waited a second for Claude to step away. "It seems like there's going to be a joint funeral. You could have just stayed out of it and saved yourself."

"Please. Let's face the marauding Huns together." Beckett paused, and I rolled my eyes. "Too much?"

"Just a little," I told him and let Beckett enter Claude's office first. Gloria sat in one of the office chairs, a coffee cup in her hand.

"Close the door," Claude said, and I did. "Well, it seems I've been somewhat blind. Gloria came in just after you left and told me I was being a damned fool."

"I did not. I said you were acting like a stupid ass." She sipped from her mug as though she'd just told everyone good morning.

"Now, let's get down to business. Payton and I have calls to make and appointments to follow up on. You have a mess to clean up."

I was on the verge of laughter, but kept my mouth shut. Claude cleared his throat and shot daggers at Gloria with his eyes. "It seems Gloria has a similar opinion to yours with regard to Garren." I nodded. "But you didn't tell me that."

"Gloria's opinion is not mine to tell," I told him. Beckett lightly touched my hand and I got the feeling my career wasn't about to be flushed down one of the agency toilets.

"See, I told you we need more people like this young man." Gloria stood. "I really think we're all done here, don't you, Claude?"

"Yes, Gloria. I think we've hammered out this issue for today."

She stood and slowly walked to the door.

"I know when I've had enough," Claude continued.

"That's good, Claude. We all want what's best for the agency." She pulled open the door and strode out. I followed, with Beckett behind me, wondering what in the hell had just happened.

Gloria paused when we reached my office, patting me on the shoulder. "I kept quiet for too long about our friend." She motioned toward Garren's closed office door. "I hoped he would grow up and become part of the team, but he never did."

"What will Claude do?" I asked.

Gloria shrugged. "You needn't worry about it." She turned to Beckett. "I'm hearing some wonderful things about you, young man. Hiram and William are impressed with your ability and work ethic. Keep it up—those things will take you far in this business." Gloria turned and took a few steps toward her office, then paused. "I tell this to all my clients, though. Don't let your head get too big. The ones who do are the assholes no one wants to deal with, and eventually they crash and burn. Happens all the time. That whole thing about nice guys finishing last is crap. Nice guys get more work. Assholes get the shaft because they're too difficult to work with." She turned away and headed toward her office, while I opened the door to mine and we stepped inside.

"You didn't have to come," I told Beckett as soon as he closed my door.

"Yes, I did. The situation you're in is as much my doing as yours." Beckett moved closer. "This isn't just about you or me—it's about us."

"Us?" I asked, a little surprised at the plural.

"Yes, us. First-person plural." Beckett smiled, and I found myself doing the same. I tried to think back over my life, and other than with my parents, I didn't think I had ever been part of an "us." "If Claude had fired you, there would have been consequences for him as well."

"I see."

"Yes. But he's a smart man."

"I somehow doubt retaining me, or you, was his sole motivation. In fact, I think Gloria had a lot to do with what happened."

"I think you underestimate your value to everyone in your life, and it's time you stopped doing that. It's time we stopped doing that. You and I are going places—me on the stage, and you in the theater business. We'll do it together." Beckett kissed me gently and pulled back. "If I do any more than that, I'm afraid things will happen that shouldn't happen in a place of business." Beckett checked his watch. "I need to get going. I have some final fittings and then run-throughs. We're working up to final rehearsals, and I'm going to be busy all week."

"I know. But it's important," I told him. "So you do your best, and I'll be waiting for you when you're done at night." I hugged him, resting my head on his chest. "Now go on and make some magic. I have some out-of-work actors who are hoping and praying that I'll be able to find them the job of a lifetime." I smiled, and Beckett grinned at me. He kissed me once before opening the door and hurrying out of my office so he wouldn't be late. I sat behind my desk and sighed like a teenager before getting to work.

"That's quite a young man you have," Gloria said as she stepped inside. "I saw him leave."

"Yeah, he is." I smiled like an idiot.

"Sometimes it isn't what we say that's important, but how we behave, and he was here for you. Granted, he didn't need to be here, but that wasn't the point."

"I know. Actions definitely speak louder than words."

EPILOGUE

"DAD, WE need to get going," I told him nervously through the door. It had taken me weeks to convince him to come for a visit. "The curtain doesn't wait for anyone."

"Are you sure about this?" Dad asked as he stepped out of the bathroom in his suit. I adjusted his tie for him and smiled.

"You look great, and of course I'm sure about this," I said.

"I can't get over the fact that you're dating Beckett Huntington. After all he put you through in high school." I loved my dad and didn't expect him to understand, at least not right off the bat. He needed some time and a chance to see that Beckett wasn't the same person he'd been in high school.

"I had trouble with that too. But, Dad—" I turned around. "I'm not the same as I was then either. There's a lot less of me. That's why I wanted you to come for a visit. I've been dating him for more than two months, and he loves me."

Dad's eyes narrowed. "You're sure about that."

I chuckled. He and I had had similar conversations multiple times over the past weeks. "To be honest, I had a hard time believing it too. But through all my fears, he was there. I even pushed him away and he came back. He thinks I'm hot, Dad."

"Too much information," he said, putting his hands over his ears with a grin.

"I know, but do you have any idea how long I waited for someone to think I was attractive?"

"You were always attractive," Dad said firmly, and I loved him for it, then and now. He'd always had faith in me. "But I'll give him the benefit of the doubt."

"Thanks, Dad," I said as I hugged him.

"Now about this apartment…. It's so small."

"It's New York, and I have the patio area." A space my dad had enjoyed for most of the previous evening. Fall was approaching, and I needed to figure out what I was going to do with the furnishings. Probably cover everything and put the cushions and rug in plastic bags. That should work. Beckett and I had talked about either getting a place together or him moving in here, but we hadn't made any decisions yet. Though I suspected the people he'd been living with were ready for him to move on—not that he'd been spending much time there.

"I get it," Dad said. He kept looking around as though he would find a door to another room at any moment.

"Let's go. We need to walk to the corner to get a cab."

"Is Val coming with us?"

"No. He has a date tonight." Val was still seeing Lars, and they seemed to be getting along. Lars was very nice. Val said they were taking things slowly, which was a change, but he said the whole mess with Rod had made him realize he needed to act differently if he wanted a different result. I couldn't argue with him. "Val has seen the play already."

I had wanted my father to come for opening night, but he already had plans.

"Then let's go." Dad headed for the door. I grabbed my keys and locked the door before leaving the building. We strolled the short distance to the curb, and I had no difficulty hailing a cab. Ten minutes later I paid the driver as we got out. I texted Beckett that we had arrived.

"The line forms along the sidewalk," a large man said, marshaling the crowd of people there to see the play. Beckett's play was a huge hit. Nearly every performance had sold out to the last seat, and the run had been extended two additional weeks. Shows were lining up for Beckett, and there was even buzz around a Tony nomination.

One of the doors cracked open, and I saw Beckett poke his head out. "Charlie, they're with me." He turned and ushered us into the lobby, the doors closing quickly behind us.

Beckett hugged me immediately. "I can't stay long. I have a few things I have to do to get ready." Beckett released me and turned to my father. "It's good to see you, Mr. Gowan. I'm glad you could make it."

A young man came up and quietly said, "Mr. Huntington, we're opening the doors in two minutes, and you're needed backstage."

"Thank you," Beckett said. He turned back to us. "I made reservations for after the show."

"Isn't there a wrap party?" Dad asked.

"We've been going so hard for so long that we decided to do it on Tuesday when we can take a little more time to celebrate." Beckett turned. "I'll see you after the show." He hurried away, and I motioned Dad to the bar, figuring we might as well get a drink.

The doors opened and the crowd filed in. Excitement filled the air as more and more people packed in.

"This is my second performance. I couldn't let the show close without seeing it again."

"I heard they are going to make a movie," my dad said.

A woman bumped me gently as I guided my dad out of the way and toward one of the ushers. We were shown our seats and sat down, sipping our drinks, as the theater began to fill.

"He seems very nice."

"He is, Dad. Beckett went through a lot of what I did, just differently." I sipped my beer and glanced over at Dad, who shrugged. "All I'm asking is that you give him a chance."

"Of course I will," Dad told me. We grew quiet as the theater filled and the excitement built. I loved this part of any performance: the anticipation. Finally, the lights flashed and then dimmed and the curtain lifted.

Just like when I'd come to the performance on opening night, I sat riveted to my chair. The play was wonderful, and I couldn't take my eyes off Beckett. I watched the play, but whenever he was on stage, he captured my attention and my gaze refused to wander to anyone else.

By the time the curtain fell, I was breathless and blinking away tears of joy and pride.

"That was amazing," Dad said from next to me as we stood, adding to the standing ovation. Tingles ran up my spine as I watched Beckett take his bow, the applause increasing. When the curtain went down for the last time, my hands and arms ached. The theater grew quieter and then filled with overlapping conversations as it emptied.

"We can stay behind," I said to Dad as I texted Beckett about where we should meet him.

In the lobby, he answered, and I led Dad out to where the bar was being put to bed and the souvenirs were getting packed away. This was the end, and it felt like it. The theater would go into rehearsals for a new show, and this one would pass into memory.

"Pay," I heard float over the work noise, and I guided Dad to where Beckett waited in dress pants and a simple white shirt, looking simply amazing.

"You remember Kendall," Beckett said, and I thought my dad was going to plotz right there. He loved Kendall's movies, so I knew this was a treat.

"Did you like the show?" Kendall asked my dad while Beckett slipped an arm around my waist.

"Yes. It was great. You were both wonderful," Dad said.

I leaned my head on Beckett's shoulder. "It was just as amazing as opening night," I said. Dad and Kendall were talking, so I took a few minutes to bask in Beckett's glow and heat.

"So what's next?" Beckett asked me.

"I've fielded a lot of offers, and we can review them on Monday and lay out a path," I told him quietly. "There's even the possibility of a movie."

"I have to meet Johnny for dinner," Kendall said, shaking hands with all of us, Beckett last. "I know we'll be working together again." Kendall said good-bye and left the lobby.

"Can you go?" I asked Beckett.

"Yes. They said we need to get our things tomorrow. I just want to eat and then go to bed." Beckett kissed me with a hint of exactly what he wanted.

Dad cleared his throat. "Should I get a hotel?"

Beckett and I shared and look. I wished I'd thought of that. "No, Dad. We'll be fine."

After leaving the theater, we walked to where Beckett said he'd made his reservations. It was French and had a longstanding theatrical tradition.

"So, I have to ask. Do you really love my son?" Dad asked Beckett. I tripped slightly on the sidewalk, and Beckett caught me, keeping me from falling.

"Dad...," I scolded.

"I want to know, and the best way is to hear it from him."

"Yes, I do," Beckett said. We stopped at a corner, waiting for the light to change so we could cross Eighth Avenue. "You saw all the excitement and energy of tonight. I love it and can't imagine doing anything else, but I'd give all of that up for Pay. The attention, the applause, the thrill of being on stage." The light changed, and we crossed with the others who had waited. "All of that is less important to me than he is."

Dad said nothing, and when we reached the other side, Beckett guided me out of the crowd while Dad moved on toward the restaurant.

"Did you mean that?" I asked.

"Yes," Beckett whispered, and I was speechless. "You are everything to me. The audience, the praise—all of it pales in comparison to the way you look at me." Beckett kissed me, pulling me into his arms.

Now *that*, I knew, was love.

ANDREW GREY grew up in western Michigan with a father who loved to tell stories and a mother who loved to read them. Since then he has lived all over the country and traveled throughout the world. He has a master's degree from the University of Wisconsin-Milwaukee and now works full-time on his writing. Andrew's hobbies include collecting antiques, gardening, and leaving his dirty dishes anywhere but in the sink (particularly when writing). He considers himself blessed with an accepting family, fantastic friends, and the world's most supportive and loving husband. Andrew currently lives in beautiful historic Carlisle, Pennsylvania.

E-mail: andrewgrey@comcast.net

Website: www.andrewgreybooks.com

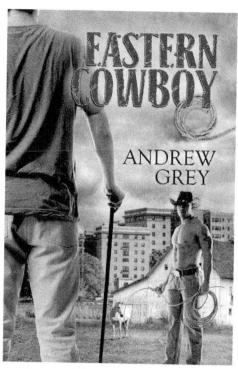

Brighton McKenzie inherited one of the last pieces of farmland in suburban Baltimore. It has been in his family since Maryland was a colony, though it has lain fallow for years. Selling it for development would be easy, but Brighton wants to honor his grandfather's wishes and work it again. Unfortunately, an accident left him relying on a cane, so he'll need help. Tanner Houghton used to work on a ranch in Montana until a vengeful ex got him fired because of his sexuality. He comes to Maryland at the invitation of his cousin and is thrilled to have a chance to get back to the kind of work he loves.

Brighton is instantly drawn to the intensely handsome and huge Tanner—he's everything Brighton likes in a man, though he holds back because Tanner is an employee, and because he can't understand why a man as virile as Tanner would be interested in him. But that isn't the worst of their problems. They have to face the machinations of Brighton's aunt, Tanner's ex suddenly wanting him back, and the need to find a way to make the farm financially viable before they lose Brighton's family legacy.

www.dreamspinnerpress.com

On the train from Lancaster to Philadelphia, Trent runs into Brit, his first love and the first man to break his heart. They've both been through a lot in the years since they parted ways, and as they talk, the old connection tenuously strengthens. Trent finally works up the nerve to call Brit, and their rekindled friendship slowly grows into the possibility for more. But both men are shadowed by their pasts as they explore the path they didn't take the first time. If they can move beyond loss and painful memories, they might find their road leads to a second chance at happiness.

A story from the Dreamspinner Press 2015 Daily Dose package "Never Too Late."

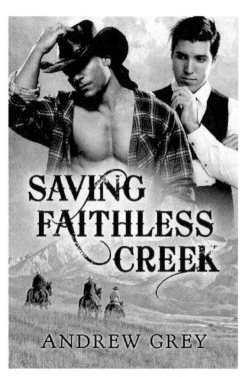

SAVING FAITHLESS CREEK

ANDREW GREY

Blair Montague is sent to Newton, Montana, to purchase a ranch and some land for his father. It's a trip he doesn't want to make. But his father paid for his college education in exchange for Blair working for him in his casinos, so Blair has no choice. When he finds out he'll be dealing with Royal Masters, the man who bullied him in high school, he is shocked. Then Blair is surprised when he finds that Royal's time in the Marines has changed him to the point where Blair could be attracted to him… if he's willing to take that chance.

Royal's life hasn't been a bed of roses. He saw combat in the military that left him scarred, and not just on the outside. When he inherits his father's ranch, he discovers his father wasn't a good manager and the ranch is in trouble. The sale of land would put them back on good footing, but he is suspicious of Blair's father's motives, and with good reason. The attraction between them is hard for either to ignore, but it could all evaporate once the land deal is sealed.

www.dreamspinnerpress.com

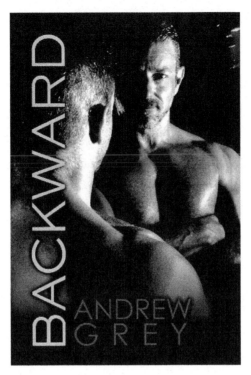

Sequel to Upside Down
Bronco's Boys: Book Three

Club owner Harry Klinger has had his eye on Tristan Martin for months, but never had the nerve to approach him. He's watched as Tristan dated Eddie and then reluctantly sat on the sidelines during the emotional breakup when Tristan discovered Eddie was dealing drugs. Now that Tristan seems to be healing, Harry hopes to get his chance.

When Eddie sends his men into Harry's club to harass Tristan, Harry steps in to help. Tristan is reluctant at first since he admittedly has terrible taste in men, but Harry seems genuine, and Tristan can't help but think Harry's sexy as well and begins to hope for happiness for both of them.

Unfortunately, Eddie isn't behaving rationally, sampling too much of his own product. With his determination to take Tristan back, it'll take more than Harry's help to keep Tristan safe as Eddie ratchets up his attempts to get what he wants.

www.dreamspinnerpress.com

FIRE AND *Ice*

ANDREW GREY

Carlisle Cops: Book Two

Carter Schunk is a dedicated police officer with a difficult past and a big heart. When he's called to a domestic disturbance, he finds a fatally injured woman, and a child, Alex, who is in desperate need of care. Child Services is called, and the last man on earth Carter wants to see walks through the door. Carter had a fling with Donald a year ago and found him as cold as ice since it ended.

Donald (Ice) Ickle has had a hard life he shares with no one, and he's closed his heart to all. It's partly to keep himself from getting hurt and partly the way he deals with a job he's good at, because he does what needs to be done without getting emotionally involved. When he meets Carter again, he maintains his usual distance, but Carter gets under his skin, and against his better judgment, Donald lets Carter guilt him into taking Alex when there isn't other foster care available. Carter even offers to help care for the boy.

Donald has a past he doesn't want to discuss with anyone, least of all Carter, who has his own past he'd just as soon keep to himself. But it's Alex's secrets that could either pull them together or rip them apart—secrets the boy isn't able to tell them and yet could be the key to happiness for all of them.

www.dreamspinnerpress.com

Hunter Wolf is a highly paid Las Vegas escort with a face and body that have men salivating and paying a great deal for him to fulfill their fantasies. He keeps his own fantasies to himself, not that they matter.

Grant is an elementary-school teacher who works miracles with his summer school students. He discovered his gift while in high school, tutoring Hunter, a fellow student. They meet again when Hunter rescues Grant in a club. Grant doesn't know Hunter is an escort or that they share similarly painful pasts involving family members' substance abuse.

After the meeting, Hunter invites Grant to one of the finest restaurants in Las Vegas. Hunter is charming, sexy, and gracious, and Grant is intrigued. With more in common than they realized, the two men decide to give a relationship a try. At first, Grant believes he can deal with Hunter's profession and accepts that Hunter will be faithful with his heart if not his body. Both men find their feelings run deeper than either imagined. For Grant, it's harder than he thought to accept Hunter's occupation, and Hunter's feelings for Grant now make work nearly impossible. But Hunter's choice of profession comes with a price, which could involve Grant's job and their hearts—a price that might be too high for either of them to pay.

www.dreamspinnerpress.com

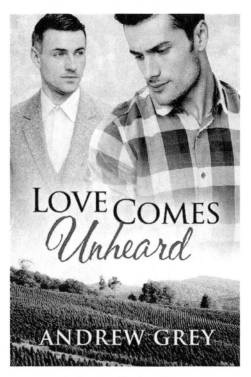

LOVE COMES
Unheard

ANDREW GREY

A Senses Series Story

Garrett Bowman is shocked that fate has brought him to a family who can sign. He's spent much of his life on the outside looking in, even within his biological family, and to be accepted and employed is more than he could have hoped for. With Connor, who's included him in his family, Garrett has found a true friend, but with the distant Brit Wilson Haskins, Garrett may have found something more. In no time, Garrett gets under Wilson's skin and finds his way into Wilson's heart, and over shared turbulent family histories, Wilson and Garrett form a strong bond.

Wilson's especially impressed with the way Garrett's so helpful to Janey, Connor and Dan's daughter, who is also deaf. When Wilson's past shows up in the form of his brother Reggie, bringing unscrupulous people to whom Reggie owes money, life begins to unravel. These thugs don't care how they get their money, what they have to do, or who they might hurt. Without the strength of love and the bonds of

www.dreamspinnerpress.com

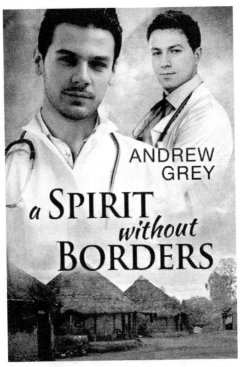

ANDREW GREY

a SPIRIT *without* BORDERS

Sequel to *A Heart Without Borders*
Without Borders: Book Two

Dillon McDowell, an infectious disease specialist, jumps at the opportunity to work with Doctors Without Borders in Liberia. But when he arrives, things are very different than he expected, and he's out of his depth. Will Scarlet takes him under his wing and helps him adjust. A hint of normalcy comes when a group of local boys invite Dillon to play soccer.

Will's family rejected him for being gay, and he's closed off his heart. Even though meeting Dillon opens him to the possibility of love, he's wary. They come from different worlds, and Will plans to volunteer for another stint overseas. But Will realizes what Dillon means to him when Dillon becomes ill, and they can no longer deny their feelings.

When Dillon's soccer friends lose their parents and aunt to disease, Will and Dillon must work together to ensure that the boys aren't cast adrift in a society that's afraid they might be contagious. They must also decide if their feelings are real or just the result of proximity and hardship.

www.dreamspinnerpress.com

Read more from this author!

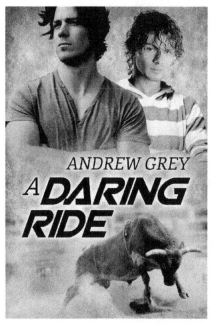

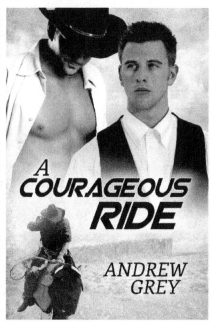

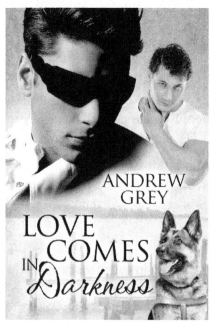

Read more from this author!

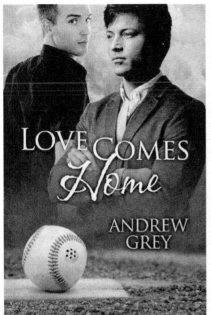

Read more from this author!

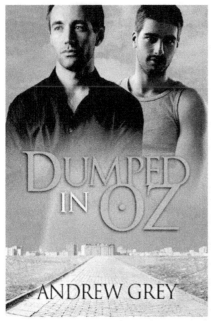
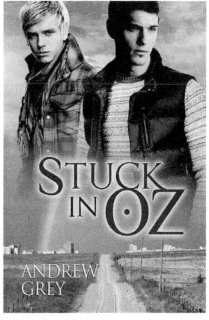
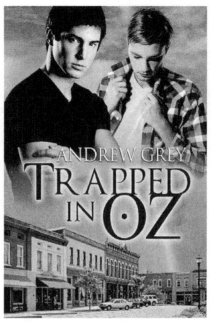

Read more from this author!

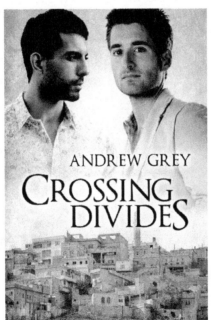

Read more from this author!

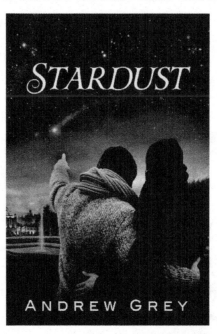

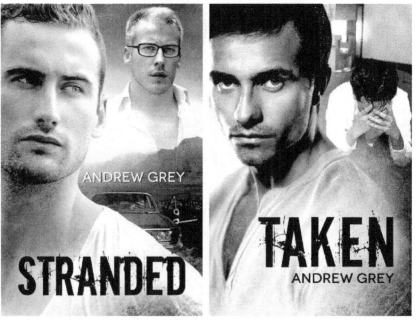

www.dreamspinnerpress.com

Read more from this author!

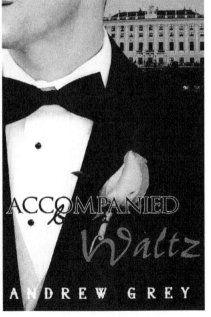

www.dreamspinnerpress.com

Read more from this author!

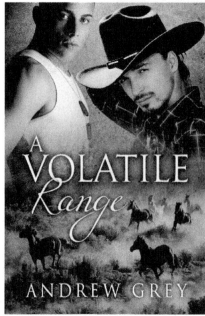

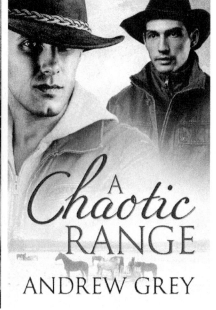

Read more from this author!

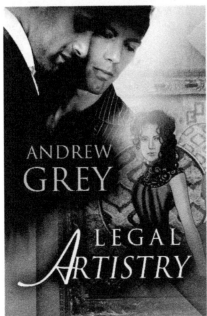
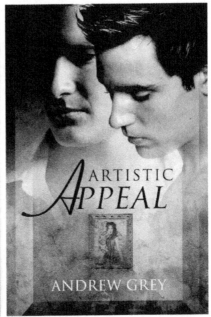

Read more from this author!

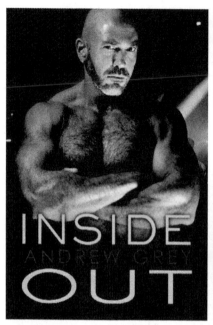

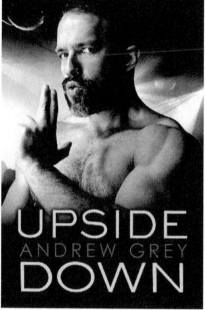

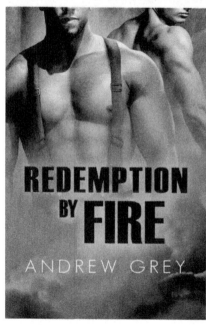

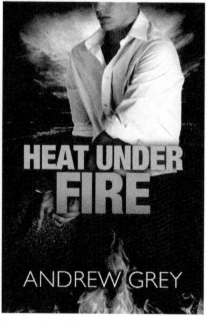

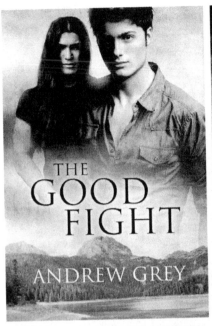
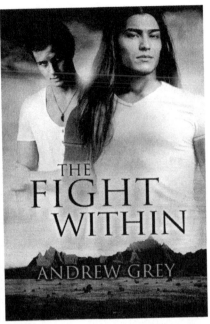

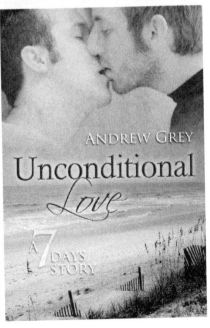

Read more from this author!

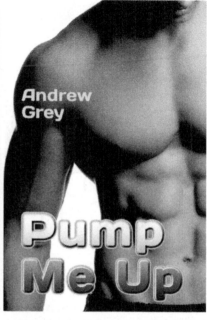

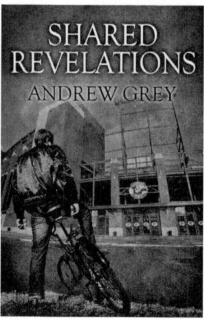